TAKE ME TO THE EDGE

KACI ROSE

Five Little Roses Publishing

COPYRIGHT

Book Cover By: **KiWi Cover Design Co.**

Editing By: Debbe @ **On The Page, Author and PA Services**

DEDICATION

To all those who ever think of running off to the mountain and leaving everyday life behind, even just for a weekend.

CONTENTS

GET FREE BOOKS!

Do you like Military Men? Best friends brothers?
What about sweet, sexy, and addicting books?

If you join Kaci Rose's Newsletter you get these books free!

https://www.kacirose.com/free-books/

Now on to the story!

CHAPTER 1

STORM

I've never been more grateful to my step-dad for always making me keep a funeral suit in my closet. While I'm grateful to have it, I'm completely heartbroken that I have to wear it today.

Standing at the graveside watching my best friend, Jason, be lowered to the ground as a 21-gun salute goes off in Arlington National Cemetery, I feel like I can't breathe. This man should be here with his wife. They are getting ready to have a child. Instead, he lost his life on his most recent deployment. Now his wife, River, is a military widow and getting ready to raise a child on her own.

If it weren't for the promise that I made him before our first deployment together, she would have absolutely no one in the world because she has no family. But I pledged to him I would take care of her if anything were to ever happen to him. That's a promise I intend to keep.

So, as I stand beside her and offer her some support as we bury her husband. At the same time, trying not to let my grief overtake me. I'm making plans to bring River back to my cabin in Whiskey River, Montana.

When I look over at River, tears are running down her face, but she's not actively sobbing. Other than the tears, her face is void of emotion. I can't imagine what's running through her mind, nor what she must be going through right now. I just hope that I can take some of the stress off her plate and do right by my best friend.

As the ceremony finishes and everyone heads out, they say goodbye to River and try to offer some words that they think will help. I stay at her side until the last person is gone. Thankfully, no one will gather back at her place and try to make small talk and fill her freezer with food.

The ceremony itself was a carefully designed performance. It was absolutely beautiful, and completely choreographed. The men and women who helped lay my friend to rest will forever hold my gratitude.

"We can sit here for as long as you like," I tell her once everyone's gone as she stares at the casket holding her husband.

She doesn't say a word. Then a moment later, she stands and walks over to the black iron stake that has his name on it temporarily until the gravestone arrives and places a hand on it.

"After the baby's born, I'd like to come back to see the headstone and introduce him to his child," she says after a moment.

"I will make that happen. As soon as the doctor clears you and your child to fly, I will bring you out here for a few days." I tell her already making plans in my head.

Anything to keep my mind off the reality of the situation right now.

She nods her head and doesn't have to ask anything more because she knows my word is as good as gold. It always has been. She also knows the promise that I made to her husband now extends to her. If this is what she needs to help get her through this dark period in her life, then I'll make sure she has it.

"I'll give you a few minutes. If you need anything, I'll be just down the row at the road. I'll be in earshot," I say. Then I leave to give her some privacy.

I wait by the road, and she joins me a few minutes later.

"Let's go home," she says. But then gives a bitter laugh. "I guess it's not really home. Not when the military can kick you out so soon after your husband dies for his country."

I don't say anything because I completely agree with her. She and Jason lived on base in military housing while he served with the United States Marines. Most young couples do because they don't have to pay rent or utilities or any maintenance on the place. Plus, your neighbors are other military families. Single guys like me ended up in the barracks, which weren't too bad, but I would definitely take Jason's place over sharing a room with another guy any day.

Once Jason was killed in action, they served her with a thirty-day notice to be out of military housing. She doesn't even get time to grieve. Instead, she has to pack up and figure out what to do with her entire life. I tried to get her more time, but all they could say was their hands were tied because there was a waitlist of families that needed the house.

Thankfully, she has a place to go. She can move back in with me. Though it didn't take much convincing to get her to agree. I think she's ready to put away all the bad memories this place now holds.

"You'll make a new home. One that no one can take away from you, one that your child will have all their firsts in, and one that you will be happy in," I tell her as I open the truck door for her and wait until she is settled.

Without saying anything else, she buckles up and stares straight ahead. I close the car door, take a deep breath, and walk around to get into Jason's truck that we drove today. She's selling the truck and wanted to take one last ride in it. As much as I didn't want to drive my friend's truck, I wouldn't deny her this either.

Once we get back to her house on base, she stands there and looks around at everything. Nothing's been touched, and the only signs that she's moving are the stack of boxes, bubble wrap, and tape in the corner that we will use for packing.

"We can sell all the furniture. The only thing that I want to keep is the crib that Jason picked out and delivered right after he found out we were expecting. It's still in the box, so it should be easy to pack in the truck," she says, standing in the entryway.

"We can bring everything with us if you want, and you can decide later. There's a storage unit in town, and I've already called and reserved three of their biggest units. I also think you should reconsider and bring Jason's truck and sell your car. The truck is going to be more useful in Montana, and it's not too late for me to get a car tow, so you don't have to drive it the whole way there."

It's a conversation that completely avoids the funeral we just attended, but at the same time talks about all the work we have ahead of us.

"I'll think about it. When would you have to call the moving company to add on the car tow?"

"I already reserved one, so it'll be there. If you don't need it, we can always take it off the reservation."

She nods with a small smile. "You're just like him, you know. Always planning ahead and one step ahead of me."

She sets her stuff down and goes to the kitchen.

"What would you like for dinner?" She asks me without even looking at me.

"How about you let me worry about dinner? Go change out of that dress and maybe run a bath. Take the night off tonight and just be. We can dive into all this again tomorrow," I tell her.

Nodding, she closes the refrigerator and slips out of her heels that she's wearing.

"Would you mind starting on Jason's office tonight? I can't bring myself to go in there. But I know the paperwork that I need to file for benefits is in there, and who knows what else. To be honest, I'm not even sure what I'm looking for."

River and Jason were one of the lucky few to get a two-bedroom military home without having a child. So, Jason used the second bedroom as an office with the intention of turning it into the baby's nursery when he returned home from deployment.

When he called me to tell me that River was pregnant, his mind was racing. He was so excited and listed off everything he planned to do as soon as he got home. My eyes burn as I remember that phone call. I have to look up at the ceiling, so the tears don't start to fall.

I can't cry in front of River. I have to be the strong one for her.

"Yeah, I can do that as long as you promise you'll relax tonight. These last few days have been plenty stressful on you, and you need to think about the baby."

Agreeing with me, she grabs a bottle of water and heads back to her room. I know jack shit about babies and pregnancy. In fact, the most experience I have is visiting the hospital after my friend Bennett and his wife Willow had their child. It was just a few days after I got the call about Jason being killed in action.

When I told my friends that I'd be bringing River home with me, it was my friend Axel's wife, Emelie who told me that stress was bad for the baby. She said to try to alleviate as much stress from her as possible over the process. So that's my goal, to take on as much of the burden as I can so that River can relax.

Removing my suit jacket and unbuttoning the sleeves of the shirt I was wearing underneath it, I go into the kitchen. Finding everything I need to make chicken parmesan for dinner, I get to work.

I can't let my mind wander off to my buddy again and what happened today, so I start making a list of everything that needs to be done. Top priority is to find the paperwork that she needs so that she can file for her benefits as soon as we get back to Whiskey River.

Through the military, she and her child will have health insurance. In addition, her child will have education benefits, and they will also get a very hefty life insurance policy of $500,000. The only downside is all the paperwork that has to be done.

Since she'll keep her medical coverage, all her doctor's visits for this pregnancy will be taken care of, but she probably won't see the life insurance money until around the time the baby is born. It will take some time for the paperwork to be approved and when they actually issue her the money.

On top of that, her child has Social Security benefits, and there are a whole other slew of things that need to be addressed.

Over dinner, neither one of us really talks about anything substantial.

"We can get rid of the dishes and the pots and pans since you'll have some of that at your house. Feel free to take any kitchen stuff that you need." She taps her fork against her plate.

"Are you sure you don't want to pack it up and bring it with us? You'll need something when you start over."

"Every item in this house holds a memory. Of course, there are things I'll take with me, but I need to start over if I'm going to be able to put one foot in front of the other and raise our child. I can't be assaulted with a memory of Jason everywhere I turn, or I'll never be able to get out of bed." She looks up at me, and her eyes are pleading with me to understand.

There are fresh, unshed tears in her eyes. It's obvious that she was crying in the bath that she took as I was making dinner. But hell, she knows there's not anything I wouldn't do for her right now.

"As you wish. When you're ready, I will make sure that you have everything that you need." Again, she just nods, knowing there's no use in fighting me for it.

After dinner, she helps by drying the dishes and putting them away since I'm still not quite sure where everything goes. Ask me where one of Jason's tools is, and I can grab it for you no problem. But of all the time that I was in this house, I avoided the kitchen because that was River's domain.

"I think I'm going to go to bed. Exhaustion hit me really hard, and I'd really like to just put today behind me." She tells me once the last dish is put away.

"Go get some sleep. I know your whole world has been turned upside down, but as long as I'm here, you're safe. I will make sure of it."

Again, she doesn't say anything. Then, hesitating, she turns to me, and the next thing I know, she's wrapping her arms around my waist for a hug. This isn't something that we do. I think the only time I have ever hugged this woman was when Jason and I came home from our first deployment, and I was just so damn excited to see someone other than Jason.

Gently, I wrap my arms around her. She's so tiny, barely five feet four to my six feet two inches. After a moment, she pulls away, and I'm left standing there wondering what the hell happened.

I've known this woman for five years now, and I've never seen her as anything more than a little sister and my best friend's wife. So why the hell am I hard as nails from just a hug?

CHAPTER 2

RIVER

All morning I've spent going through my closet sorting out the clothes that I wanted to keep. I'm trying to figure out what I want to do with Jason's. I pulled out one of his sweatshirts, but I've packed up everything else. Not having the heart to get rid of it just yet, I will put them all into storage.

Somehow, I will find a way to use them for our child. Whether it's making them into a blanket or some other item, I'll make it work because I want our child to feel as close to their father as possible. Needing a break, I head to Jason's office to see what progress Storm is making.

But I stop at the doorway as I just can't bring myself to walk into the room. I find Storm sitting on the floor with his back to the wall, staring at a framed photo in his hand.

"What's that?" I ask, startling him.

He looks over at me, giving me a sad smile, and for the first time since he's gotten here, I can see some emotion on his face.

"I've never seen this picture," he says, showing it to me.

It's a photo I took of Jason and him when they got back from their second deployment together. Jason had been deployed for his twenty-first birthday, so Storm took him out to a bar and ordered some crazy shots. The photo is of them throwing back the first one. Jason's first legal drink.

"He loved that photo, and I snapped it completely randomly. I was just thinking to capture the moment. He'd want you to have that. To remember the good times." I try to smile, but I can tell that it's wobbly. "And don't be afraid to show emotion around me. Actually, it will be nice knowing I'm not the only one constantly on the verge of tears."

Then I turn to go back to my room.

"Hey, River?" he says.

At his words, I stop to look at him.

"You're not the only one constantly wanting to cry. But I refuse to break down here, not like this. I'll hold it together until we get home, back to Whiskey River, where I know I'm safe, and I know you're safe."

Like with many of his statements, I never know what to say, so I just nod and head back to my room. I pull down a few boxes that are on the top shelf in the bedroom, boxes that hold Christmas, fall, and Halloween decorations.

Setting them all on the bed, I open them up one by one. Most of these are things that I would pick up when I was shopping at the exchange or off the clearance rack to use the following year.

None of the decorations hold much appeal anymore except for the box that has our

Christmas decorations. Mixed in with our Christmas decorations are ornaments that we bought, celebrating different parts of our relationship. Some of them start all the way back to when we were just friends in high school.

The letter A is from the year that I got all straight A's. The night sky ornament goes with our prom theme, which was a night under the stars, and it's also the night we went to prom together. I even made an ornament with the dried rose petals he scattered on the bed the first time that we slept together. There's one from our wedding and every Christmas from the time we started dating. Every time he was deployed from each place he visited, he brought back an ornament.

These I want to keep. If nothing else, my child deserves these. I couldn't care less about the Christmas lights that would take us all day to untangle, and he would curse up a storm putting up. Or the Christmas tree that we never could get to look full enough after being in a box all year.

Carefully I pack the ornaments up and then take the boxes of the decorations and set them in the pile in the living room of items that will go to donation. Storm tried to talk me into doing a yard sale to try to make some money off of this stuff, but I don't think I would physically be able to sell it to someone. Donating it and knowing that it will do some good to help the local Children's Hospital makes it a lot easier to give away.

When I'm back to my room pulling out a few boxes from under my bed, I hear a knock at the front door. I freeze in absolute terror.

The last time there was a knock on the door, two men in uniform informed me that my husband was dead.

"You are expecting anyone?" Storm asks as he steps into the hallway. I just shake my head.

He goes to the front door, and I follow him, stepping out of the hallway just far enough so I can see the door. He looks back at me before he opens it. There's a man in uniform standing next to a man in jeans and a T-shirt. Neither of which I've ever seen before.

"We are looking for River Owens., the man in uniform says.

Storm doesn't budge, but I take a step forward to get a better look at their faces. Though neither of them looks familiar.

"That's me," I say, while trying to look around Storm who still hasn't moved out of their way.

"We're here to deliver this summons to you." The one not in uniform says, and that seems to capture Storm's attention. He snatches the envelope out of the man's hand.

"Anything else?" he growls.

The two men just stand there shaking their heads. So he slams the door in their face before turning and walking over to me.

Taking my hand, he leads me to the couch and sits down next to me, handing me the envelope. My hands are shaking so much that he takes the envelope back and opens it before handing it back to me.

Pulling it out, we read the paper together. The paper informs me that there is a court order for me to submit to a DNA test per Jason's parent's demands. A piercing chill starts scrolling up my spine, and my chest feels heavy. Every breath feels like a weight that is pulling me deeper into a dark hole.

I grip my chest, trying to ease the pressure as my vision starts to narrow. There's a ringing in my ears, and I can't hear anything around me other than my heart racing like a wild animal. No matter how much I try, I can't seem to get more than a short gasp of air.

Storm is on his knees in front of me, gripping my arms. His mouth is moving, but I hear nothing. All I can do is grip onto him for dear life as a piercing panic takes over me. I've never felt anything like this in my life.

Jason's parents don't think the child is his. The fact they think so low of me that I would cheat on their son fills me with nothing but disgust. It feels like ice is running through my veins, and I start to shake uncontrollably and shiver as the room closes in on me.

Storm grips my face with his hands and angles my head as he locks eyes with me. Something about the connection seems to slowly push the ice back and break the chains which were stopping me from breathing.

"Take a deep breath with me," Storm says.

Matching my breathing to his, I focus on nothing but my breath.

While still taking deep breaths, he pulls the blanket off the back of the couch and wraps it around me. Then he rubs his hands up and down my arms like he's trying to warm me up. Once I can breathe again, there's only one emotion that takes over, and I start to cry uncontrollably.

Storm sits on the couch beside me and pulls me into his arms. He tucks my head into his neck and lets me sob. He doesn't tell me to stop crying or that everything's going to be okay. Instead, he just rubs my back and lets me get it all out. This is really the first time that I've cried since the funeral a few days ago.

I don't know how long we sit there, but I don't want to move. Eventually, I find his hand gently rubbing my back, which helps me stop crying.

"This is all my fault," I say without even lifting my head.

"There is no way this is your fault," Storm says.

It sounds like he's shocked I could even think something like that.

"No, it is. When I found out about Jason, I wrote them. I thought maybe they'd want to be at the funeral. That just maybe they want to be in their grandkid's life. I don't know what I was thinking. Even though I've never interacted with them much, Jason's told me all about them. I guess I was hoping against hope for even the slightest bit of a family."

Storm doesn't have to say anything. It's as clear as day that there's a reason Jason didn't have contact with his parents anymore. They weren't thrilled with him joining the military, but they completely cut him out of his life when he married me. I don't feel guilty about it because Jason made it very clear that he loved me, and when he promised to always take care of me, I knew he meant it. Besides, I may not have a family, but I do know I could never turn my back on my child based on who they loved.

Then the thought hits me, and I can feel the panic starting back up again.

"Is a DNA test even safe for the baby right now?" I ask. All I know of DNA tests are the cheek swabs. How are they going to get to the baby's cheek without puncturing the placenta?

"Hey, hey, calm down. Deep breaths. There's no need to have another panic attack over this. I don't think the court would have ordered it if it wasn't safe. But let's do a little research before we head down that road, okay?" Storm wraps one arm around my shoulders and pulls me to his side while using the other hand to take out his phone and research.

Completely worn out, I rest my head on his shoulder and read the articles on his phone that he keeps pulling up.

"So, it looks like to do the DNA test all they need is a simple blood draw from you," Storm says. Then he goes on to explain some science stuff about floating fetal DNA and how the whole thing works. Right now, all this information just makes my head spin.

"You're absolutely certain that this is safe for the baby?" I ask because I'm in no head space for this.

"Absolutely! Otherwise, I'd help you fight it. But I am going to make a suggestion. It says you need to report within the next seven days for this test. I think we should do the test and then leave the next morning," he says.

Even though he doesn't give his reasonings, they hang in the air. Because we both know if Jason's parents are asking for a DNA test, something is brewing.

Especially since there has been zero contact from them before. This means they've pulled some strings from some of their wealthy influential connections to get this pushed through.

I don't answer right away because even though I know he's right, that means I've got to get my ducks in a row, and I'm already making plans.

"I have a four-bedroom cabin and plenty of room. Let's just pack everything up, and you can sort it all out there. We need to get you out of here."

"After I do the test, we can leave. Why don't you go ahead and get this furniture listed? I don't want to take the furniture as I have no need for it. The big thing is finding the paperwork I need in Jason's office. All the rest of this can be packed up to be gone through later. But I don't think I can step foot in that office," I say, finally sitting up to look at Storm.

"I will handle the office. Pack up what you want to take to the cabin. Keep all that in your room. Anything else that is in the living room will go into storage. What about the truck?"

"Let's take it. I'll drive it."

"All right. Let me call the moving company and see about picking up everything early. I'll make the arrangements. You just start packing up your stuff. Can I take this and read over it a bit more?" he asks, holding the paper with the order for the DNA test.

Nodding, I go back to my room, and he heads to the office. But for the life of me, I have no idea what more he could get from that letter. But I know Storm, he always has a plan.

CHAPTER 3

STORM

Only as we cross the first of many state lines do I start to relax even a little bit. In the passenger seat beside me, River is fast asleep. Yesterday, about an hour before the facility closed, I took her to do the DNA test. Then, with the help of a couple of the guys that knew Jason, we loaded up the moving truck, so it was ready to go.

At the first sign of daylight this morning, I woke River up. She gathered her things, got in the truck, and went right back to sleep. I just want to put as many miles between us and Jason's parents as possible. In Montana,

I can protect her better, and that's what I intend to do.

Her mail is being forwarded to my buddy Jack's shop in town, should anything come of this. My gut has never been wrong, and my gut is screaming at me right now.

She absolutely did the right thing, letting his parents know that their son was dead and that they had a grandchild on the way. Had I been there, I would have told her not to do it. Jason and I talked a lot during deployments. We talked about our parents and knowing what I know of his parents, I wouldn't want them in my child's life.

But I also know River is clinging to any part of a family that she has left. She was a foster kid, met Jason met in middle school, and they've been inseparable ever since. He gave her the family she didn't have. Now that he's gone, I'm sure losing family is only a small part of what she's feeling.

What she's soon going to realize is that I'm her family now, and so will my friends up on the mountain be her family. And as I promised Jason, she won't ever be alone. It goes unsaid that his child will know endless amounts of love as well. River seems to think my taking care of her applies until she is back on her feet. But she'll soon see it applies for as long as I am on this Earth. That is the type of bond I had with Jason. The promise I made to him I intend to take seriously.

I'm hoping covering some distance today will avoid any more of the panic attacks that she had the day that we got served the letter for the DNA test. I've never felt so helpless in those minutes before our eyes locked, and I was able to stabilize her.

Just thinking back to it makes my gut churn. If stress isn't good for the baby, I can only imagine that a panic attack is even worse.

I've allowed us five days to get from Virginia to Montana. In addition, I made sure that she had a doctor's appointment for her and the baby in eight days. While I wanted to give her a little time to adjust to the move, I also wanted her seen quickly, especially after all of this. Thankfully, she didn't fight me on it.

My phone pings again, and a quick glance on the dashboard where I'm using it for directions shows that it's my mom. Once again, she's telling me to be safe and let her know when we get in for the night. My parents have always supported me in everything that I do. From wanting to live on the mountain and having space from everybody to keeping my promise to Jason to when I joined the military.

Being back in Montana, back around my parents gives me more power for the fight I truly believe we have coming up. My friends will give her the support system that she needs, and hopefully they will make Whiskey River feel like home to her.

"When we stop for lunch, I really need to pee," she says, her voice groggy.

Her words pull me from my thoughts. "We can stop now as I've allowed extra time because I know you're going to have to use the restroom. Plus, it's better for you to get out and stretch your legs more," I tell her just as we pass a sign for a rest stop.

She smiles at me, and while it's not the carefree huge smile she had the last time that I saw her, I'll take even the small one because it's progress from the last few days.

Once we're done, and we're heading back to the truck, she stops and looks at the truck.

"It's sad to think my whole life can fit in that thing. But I guess I should be grateful because when I met Jason my whole life could fit in the back seat of a car." She shakes her head and walks off to get into the truck.

I open the door for her, making sure she's all settled before getting in on my side.

"When I got out of the military, all I had was my truck and the clothes on my back. I never accumulated much because I lived in the barracks and was constantly deployed. I've had to furnish my cabin myself. So I get it, actually owning things hits differently."

I start up the truck as she looks at me, but doesn't say anything. We continue our journey West, and a small part of me wonders if this is what the settlers felt trying to get to Oregon. The desperate need to put distance between them and whatever they were running from, knowing that safety was just on the other side of the country.

CHAPTER 4

RIVER

The movies always romanticize road trips to be this great and wonderful thing. For the longest time, I couldn't wait to be able to go on my first road trip and buy snacks, listen to music, and sing at the top of my lungs. All the things that you see people do on road trips on TV.

Road trips while pregnant? That's different. What they don't tell you about is the constant having to stop to pee or the nauseousness of driving through the mountains while the baby is moving around. Not to mention the complete boredom of being in the car eight hours a day for five days straight. That's what they don't talk about.

Also, what they don't mention is how it leaves you plenty of time to be in your own head on whatever is going on in your life. For me, that's the death of Jason and how guilty I feel that I'm not the blubbering widow who can't get out of bed because they lost the love of their life. I loved Jason, I truly did. He was my best friend in the whole world, and I think he was my soul mate on that level. But I don't think he was my romantic soul mate.

Would I have been happy spending the rest of my life with him? Absolutely. He was safe and exactly what I needed. He treated me great, and I knew he would make an amazing father. But in the back of my head, I'd always wonder if what I read in my romance novels was true. You know, that life-changing kind of love.

I doubt I'll be able to find it now. No one's going to want to be strapped down with someone else's kid, but that doesn't mean I won't wonder.

Those are the types of thoughts that filled my head crossing the country. At the same time, I was imagining the town that I was going to be living in and what I would do. I thought about trying to make plans for my life ahead of me. And the worrying about all the paperwork I have yet to fill out, and about why Jason's parents wanted a DNA test and what they would say or do once it came back. Then they'll know that the child I'm carrying is definitely Jason's. I would never cheat on him, and he knew that. Storm knew that, too. He didn't even question it.

All I did was sit in the moving truck all day. Even though Storm did all the driving, mentally I was exhausted.

So, as we pull into the town of Whiskey River, I feel a small sense of relief.

"If you want to take a look, we're going to drive through downtown. But I promise we can come down and look around more when you have your doctor's appointment," he says.

Finally, we pull onto what looks like a Main Street with the beautiful mountains in front of us and stores and restaurants lining the streets.

There are people walking, holding shopping bags, and others sitting on tables just outside the bakery enjoying a coffee and a pastry. In one way, it looks exactly like how I'd expect a small town to look, and in another it's the complete opposite of what I expected.

You hear people in the city talk about how small towns are dying and the buildings are abandoned and rundown and yet there's not a single empty building on this street. Everything is well kept with flowers and decorations. There are benches scattered along Main Street to take in the view of the mountains, and it truly looks like something off of a postcard.

We turn onto a road just past town, and a storage unit is in front of us. There are several pickup trucks greeting us with guys just as big and as muscular as Storm. All of them have a woman with them, and I wonder if these are the friends that Storm was talking about.

Getting out of the truck, I am thankful to stretch my legs yet again. Storm walks to my side, and he introduces me to everybody, but the names are all a blur.

"They're going to help us unload the stuff that stays here in storage. Also, this is also where we are returning the truck and the car tow. So we're going to unhook your truck and drive it up the mountain to the cabin. One of the guys is going to follow us and make sure we don't have problems getting it home," Storm says.

"Oh, I'm sure it will be fine. We don't need to inconvenience them," I say as a blonde girl walks up to stand beside me with a smile on her face.

"That's not an option," the blonde woman says. "After you've been driving for five days, and everything that you've been through, you don't know this mountain yet. We will make sure you get home. You'll learn all these guys are super protective of us, and you're one of us now."

Looking at her, I'm trying so hard to remember her name. Even though Storm just introduced me, I'm pulling up a blank.

"Thank you and I'm sorry you're right. It has been several long days, and I'm horrible with names."

"I'm Emelie and don't worry. It'll take you a little bit to get them all down. We totally understand," she says with a laugh.

Then she hooks her arm in mine and leads me over to the truck that she and her husband came in. She reaches in and pulls out a white paper bag.

"We stopped at the bakery and got some of these huckleberry scones that are to die for. I thought you could use a little snack," she says, handing me the bag. I can see her husband pulling something out of the back of his truck, and when I turn around, I find him setting up a folding camping chair.

"That's his way of saying sit down and relax. Let them handle this. He's not a big talker," she says.

Going back to the truck, he pulls out another chair and sets it up right beside me.

"You too, Little One, sit down and have a break. Keep her company," he says to her.

She smiles like she just won the lottery. Standing on her tippy toes, she pulls him down for a sweet, but short kiss before sitting down and watching him walk off to join the guys. They really do make the cutest couple.

As the guys unload everything, the girls all seem to migrate over to where we are sitting. We all talk and chat, getting to know each other. Willow is easy to spot because she's the one with the newborn baby attached to her in some cloth carrier on her chest.

The girls talk about Whiskey River and about some people that I have no idea who they are. They discuss the brewery that just opened and some events happening downtown in a few weeks as well.

Before I even know it, the men are done putting everything into storage. After unhooking the truck, they join us with a few bottles of water in hand. Storm walks over to me and hands me a bottle.

"Make sure you drink. Even though it's not really hot out, it's arid. You have got to stay hydrated," he says.

Without arguing, I take the bottle and take some small sips.

"My husband and I are going to follow you up the mountain, so we'll see you shortly when you get to the cabin," Emelie says.

As we all start getting ready to head out, she gives me a hug, and Storm walks me over to the moving truck and once again helps me inside.

When the town is behind us and we're closer to the mountain, I look over at the Storm.

"Is this truck going to make it up to your cabin?" I ask worried for the first time.

I remember Jason telling me about Storm moving to a remote cabin in some small town in Montana. It suits him, and I know he's happy there. Though until now, I never gave it much thought. But seeing the actual mountain, knowing we still have to drive this truck full of all my crap through it is daunting.

"Yep, we're a lot lighter now after dropping that stuff off at storage," he says with a smile.

It's a smile that says I don't need to worry about anything because he's taking care of it.

The drive up the mountain is absolutely beautiful with the wildflowers scattered around. Every once in a while, you can make a turn and have an absolutely gorgeous scenic view. Before I know it, we are pulling off the main road and turning into a gated driveway.

Axel and Emelie follow us up the long driveway. The cabin at the end of it looks nothing like what I expected. I was thinking maybe some rundown cabin in the woods that had been used as a hunting cabin that he turned into a home. But no, this place could be on the cover of a slick cabin magazine as a model home.

It's absolutely stunning with tons of windows, and my mouth drops open as I take it in.

"Go give her the grand tour while I start unloading." Axel, Emelie's husband says.

Storm holds his hand out for me, and I hesitate for just a moment. This isn't something he's done before, so I hesitantly take his hand, and he leads me into the house. We walk into a large wide-open room, and ahead of us are two-story floor-to-ceiling windows taking advantage of the mountain view at the back of the property.

There's a large stone fireplace, and wood floors. The whole place looks like it's a resort in a hot vacation destination. Not placed in the backwoods of Montana.

"All the bedrooms are to the left, down that hallway. To the right is the large sunroom where I keep the dogs that I train. Their stuff is down that way. I will introduce you to them later," he says, guiding me down the hallway.

"This room I've mostly used for storage, but have plans to clear out so you can use it as a nursery for the baby because it's right next to your room here. This room across from you is my office, but the bathroom here in the hallway will be all yours. At the end of the hallway is my room and I have a bathroom in there." He continues giving me a short tour.

As we finish up the tour, Axel brings in a few of my bags, and he sets them in my room.

"Why don't you get a head start on unpacking, and I'll help him bring the rest of the stuff in," Storm says before heading out.

This bedroom is nothing more than a bed with nightstands on either side and a dresser. There are some curtains over the windows, but other than that, there are no decorations or thought put into the room.

It just screams the typical guy not worried about decorations, just functionality. Picking up one of my suitcases, I set it on the bed and open it. Then I unpack my clothes, putting them into the dresser.

Between all the clothes, wrapped in bubble wrap, is my framed wedding photo of Jason. At the moment, it's one of the most precious things that I have. It was the day that I finally got a family and wasn't alone.

That was the day I finally felt safe, loved, and wanted. I don't think I can remember a day I've been happier. This photo with both of us smiling at each other captures such a feeling of joy. I think about putting it on the dresser, but stop, wondering if it would be weird to set up my wedding photo while I'm living with another guy even, if that guy is Storm.

"I've always loved that photo. You just look so happy," Storm says from the doorway as he sets down another suitcase.

"Would it be weird if I set the photo up in the house?" I ask, completely unsure.

"I think it would be weirder if you didn't," he says, leaving me to finish unpacking.

Once Axel and Emelie said their goodbyes, I meet Storm in the living room. In here, he has some photos set up. One of them is of the three of us at the Marine ball. The guys are all dressed up in their suits, and I'm in one of my fancy gowns that Jason bought for me.

"Let me introduce you to the dogs. They're well behaved and super friendly. I usually let them wander around the house when I'm home," he says.

I follow him down the hallway that he pointed out earlier.

"Who took care of them while you were gone?"

"My buddy Cole and his wife Jana. You met them down at the storage unit."

The names sound familiar, but I can't put a face on them.

At the end of the hallway, there's a door with glass panes so you can see the large sunroom beyond it. There are dog beds everywhere and the dogs are lying there. Some of them are asleep, while others are looking at the door. Though I'm happy to see that none of them are charging toward the door.

When we walk in, they turn, paying attention, like they're waiting for Storm to give a command.

"How many are there?" I ask, staring at what looks like a sea of sled dogs.

"Right now, I have twelve. But those three that are lying on the far side of the room are currently pregnant. So, I'm expecting anywhere between fifteen to twenty-five puppies in the next couple of months."

We walk through the room, and he introduces me to each one, pulling treats out of his pocket. Then he proceeds to give each one a treat and a little attention. My hormones must be completely out of whack because there's something extremely sexy about watching him with these dogs that I know he's trained. I'm taken by how well they respect him.

I always thought dogs and animals, in general, were good judges of character. So the fact that he has these dogs respect says a lot about him. That must be why my hormones are raging and I'm slightly turned on watching him interact with the dogs.

"Are you okay if I let them into the house or would you rather them stay back here?" He asks once I'm introduced to everyone. Though how he tells them apart I will never know.

"This is their home, and I'm just a guest. They can absolutely be out there wandering around, especially if they're this well behaved."

As I spend the rest of the day unpacking and putting things away, there's always a dog lying in my doorway. It's as if they're watching over me for Storm. But that night when I go to bed, I leave my door open, and not one, but six dogs funnel into my room.

They scatter around on the floor, and one of them comes over and sniffs the bed.

This was one of the male dogs. I only remember because I noticed that his eyes were two different colors. Reaching over, I pet him and give a thorough rub down, but when I stop, he jumps up on the bed and lies at the foot of the bed.

"I don't know if you're allowed on the bed, but I hope you don't get in trouble with your dad." Sitting up, I pet him a little more.

"They're allowed in your room or on your bed as long as you're comfortable. If not, you just tell them so, and they'll leave. I usually have a couple that end up on my bed throughout the night as well. In the morning I will have breakfast ready for you, but sleep in as long as you'd like. Goodnight, I'm heading off to bed," Storm says, going off to his room.

I've never had a pet growing up, but I've always wanted a dog. Now I have six of them in my room. I finally understand what a few of my friends at school would say when they said that they weren't scared because they had a dog. I think this is better than any security system you could ever buy.

"Alright goodnight, guys," I say as I lie down. Each dog gives out a little ahh-ohh in response that I didn't expect.

Worried that Storm is going to get upset, I shush them. Then I hear a loud chuckle from his room.

I've always known Storm was a good guy, but he's completely different than the man I had built up in my head. Now I'm starting to wonder if moving out here with him was such a good idea.

CHAPTER 5

STORM

River has been here for a few days now, and I think we've settled into a good routine. After getting the dogs their first morning exercise, I will cook breakfast for us. That way she can sleeping in and get the rest she needs. Then she spends the day in my office either applying for jobs or doing research, figuring out her next steps, and filling out all the paperwork that needs to happen. While she's inside, I'm outside with the dogs or working around the cabin.

Since I will have two extra people to prepare for this winter, I've been working hard to get ready. She takes over making our lunch, and then after I come in and clean off, I make dinner. Even though she's tried to fight me on this one, she's been through a lot. The least I can do is try to take some of the weight off her shoulders for the next couple of weeks.

I did concede that once we talked to the doctor and she got a clean bill of health, she could start helping with dinner.

Today is to her doctor appointment. It's a morning appointment, and she agreed to let me take her out to lunch afterward. We can spend some time in town before heading back up the mountain. Tonight we're having dinner with Jenna and Phoenix, along with some of the other guys.

My buddy's wives are ready to make her feel at home and find out how they can help. So they didn't want to wait too long to have another get together, even though they just saw each other while we were on packing the stuff into her storage unit. According to Phoenix, that doesn't quite count as a proper introduction.

"This drive really is beautiful." She says as we wind through the mountain roads going into town.

"It really is. It's gorgeous after that first light dusting of snow. With the snow covering the mountains, it seems like a completely different world. But snow tends to trap us on the mountain for a few months in the winter, so you might hate the snow by spring." I've been trying to prepare her for winter on the mountain because I know that she'll be here for that.

Heck, winter here in general, even in town, will be completely different than what she's used to in Virginia.

"You know you really should plan on being with me at the cabin this winter. It's your first winter, and being pregnant, I may not be able to get down the mountain if you need me," I say, thinking out loud.

"But what if I end up needing a doctor, and we can't get down the mountain?"

"My buddy Cole lives not too far, and he can get to us even in the snow. He was a medic in the military. We went to boot camp to-gether and served on my last deployment together. He's the one who saved my life." I force myself to open up a little just so she knows that I absolutely trust this guy.

"I like that we have medical help so close. To be honest, I don't know when I'm going to be able to move out. I haven't even started looking for a job because this paperwork for the benefits is taking up most of my time."

Immediately, I drop the subject, as the last thing I want to do is stress her out be-fore her doctor's appointment. We switch to talking about more relaxing subjects like dogs. She seems absolutely fascinated by them, especially the same six dogs that sleep in her room every night.

When we get to the doctor's office, they're not really busy and get us right in. They run a few tests and have her pee in a cup. All the fun stuff since she's being established as a new patient. Then we wait for the doc-tor. I get comfortable prepared to wait for a while, but River barely has time to get settled on the exam table before the doctor is walking in.

"Hello, Mom. Oh, and hello Dad." The doctor says when she sees me.

"Oh, I'm not...." I shift in my seat, not sure how much River wants to share.

"My husband was killed on deployment, and this is our best friend who is stepping in to help because I don't have any family," she says. But looks at me with this very soft smile that makes my heart race in a way that it shouldn't.

"I am so sorry to hear that, but I'm glad you have someone who's willing to help you out. I will make a note in the chart, so it doesn't happen again. Do you want to put him down as someone we can release information to as your emergency contact and such?" the doctor asks.

River looks at me like she wants to know if I'm okay with that.

I give her a soft nod.

She smiles again. "Yeah, I would."

"Perfect. Just talk to the receptionist on the way out and they will take care of all that. Now let's talk for a moment about your stats. Your blood pressure is a little high, so I'm going to retake it to see if it's any lower. Sometimes travel and the stress of being here on time can cause it to rise."

"Or the stress from the funeral and the move across the country?" I say as the doctor hooks the blood pressure cuff up to River's arm.

"That definitely could have something to do with it, too." The doctor gives me a smile and then retakes her blood pressure.

"It is actually two points higher. Now that I know all that you're going through, my guess is you just need some rest. Let's take a listen to the baby's heartbeat, measure you, and make sure everything else looks good before we jump to any conclusions. Go ahead and lie back," the doctor says.

When I see the worry all over River's face, I go to her side and take her hand. In return, she squeezes mine for dear life.

She doesn't have to say a word with that grip. In it, I can feel the prayer of her begging me and begging the universe for her baby to be all right. I don't think I ever prayed so hard for anything myself, either. The doctor pulls out a tape measure to measure her belly. In the clothes that she wears, she doesn't show yet. But as the doctor looks up her shirt to measure, there's definitely a little swell there that you can't miss.

"You are measuring about sixteen weeks. Does that sound about right?" The doctor looks over at the River.

"Yes, sixteen weeks as of two days ago," River confirms.

I'm not sure why, but I didn't realize she was that far along.

Next, the doctor takes out what looks like a miniature karaoke machine. It's a box with a small, attached microphone. She squeezes some gel on River's stomach and then moves the microphone over it.

Different sounds fill the room. But I would not be able to tell you what any of them were. Though none of them seemed to be what the doctor's looking for. She keeps moving the microphone around. Then suddenly a loud whooshing sound fills the room, almost like a train rushing past us.

"There's your baby," the doctor says with a huge smile.

"What's wrong with it? Why is the heart-beat so fast?" I ask, instantly concerned that something's wrong.

"That is absolutely normal. A baby's average heart rate can be anywhere between 110 beats per minute to 160 beats per minute. Your baby is averaging about 150 which is perfectly normal. That means baby is happy in there."

The doctor wipes the gel off of River's belly and helps her sit up as River readjusts her clothes.

"So, looking over your chart that was faxed over and based on what you've told me, it looks like all the stress is what's causing the higher blood pressure. I'd like for you to go home and relax. Try to lie on your left side as much as possible, which will help keep the blood flowing to the baby. I know it's not possible to lie on your left side all the time, as that would be very uncomfortable. But anytime you think about it, try to be on your left side for as long as you can."

"You're putting me on bed rest?" I can hear the worry in River's voice.

"No, I don't think we have to be that drastic. But I would like you to rest as much as possible. Take a couple extra baths or maybe read a book. Don't do yard work or go for a run. Try to eliminate some of the stress out of your life over the next two weeks. You should also cut out caffeine, fried foods and limit your salt intake. Then I'll have you come back in, and we'll check your blood pressure and urine again to make sure that this isn't the start of something else," the doctor says.

We thank her and fill out the paperwork to add me to River's chart. Then I take her to lunch as planned.

"Cut out the stress after my husband dies, and I've got a million things to do," she says once we are seated at the cafe waiting for our food.

"River, I want you to understand there is absolutely no rush for you to leave. Take your time sending the paperwork in. Once that baby is born, you're going to need help. You're not meant to do it on your own. If you need to stay two to three years, I'll be fine with it. But at the very least, will you agree to stay through the birth of the baby until you both get the all clear from the doctor?"

Her eyes go wide as she looks at me. "That could be another six to nine months."

"I know. But I'm not just going to kick you out when you're not ready. God forbid something goes wrong, and you have to have a C-section and need help even longer. What I don't want is you stressing," I say as our food arrives.

"Thank you, Storm. I will agree to stay until I get the okay from the doctor. Besides, you owe me a trip to Arlington around that time, anyway," she says, smiling sadly.

"You're right, I do. And I always keep my promises. Now, as for the paperwork that seems to be causing you stress. Why don't I sit down tonight and take a look at it and see if I can't help get some or all of it done so that you can relax?"

"I want to say that I can do it, but some of the terminology takes me forever to search and figure out what it means, so I'm going to take you up on that." She digs into her grilled chicken Caesar salad.

"Since the doctor said you need to relax, walking around downtown is going to be out today. But I think we should still go down to the thrift store and see if we can find any maternity clothes for you."

As she was getting ready today, she quickly realized that most of her clothes no longer fit. So, I mentioned checking out the thrift store to see if we could find some before we make a trip into Helena. Willow said she was able to find some decent stuff there.

After we eat, we go to the thrift store, and she's able to get a pair of shorts, two pairs of jeans, and several tops. She also grabbed a few large T-shirts and a pair of sweatpants to wear around the house. As she reaches for her wallet to pay for them, I'm right there swiping my card before she gets the chance.

"Storm, I can buy my own maternity clothes," she says, looking embarrassed.

"I know you can, but I promised to take care of you, and that's what I'm going to do. Take the money and put it towards things you need for the baby." I take the bag from the cashier, and we go out to my truck.

"I wonder if we should reschedule our dinner tonight?" I say thinking out loud on the drive home.

"Please don't. We have a few hours. I promise I will lie down on the couch and watch TV and not do anything until it's time to leave. But I've been really looking forward to this dinner and getting to know your friends."

I hesitate because I want to do as the doctor says, but I also want her to make friends and connections and not feel isolated, either. "Fine, but you need to be sitting down all night. Whether it's on the couch or at the dining room table, you'll sit and put your feet up. Deal?"

"Yes, thank you."

As promised, she rests all afternoon in the living room with a few dogs standing guard. Then, before dinner time, we head to Phoenix and Jenna's house. Before we even get a chance to knock, Jenna opens the door with a welcoming smile on her face.

"Come in, come in. Storm messaged my husband and told him about your little deal. I fell in love with this chaise lounge that I saw online. Well, with my husband being amazing at making furniture, he made me an exact copy. Oh my word, it is the most comfortable thing I have ever sat on. Furniture wise anyway," Jenna says, throwing her husband a wink. "I've added a blanket and some pillows, and it is all yours for the night."

Then she takes River's hand and pulls her towards the lounge as everyone introduces themselves to her again. The guys gather on the other side of the room at the dining room table, where we can still see the girls but gives them enough space to have their girl talk time.

"So, how's it going having a pregnant woman in your house?" Cole asks.

"It's not bad. I know hormones aren't in full swing yet, but the dogs are protective of her, and I don't mind her in my space."

A few of the guys exchange looks.

"What are those looks for?" I ask, even though I'm not sure I want to know.

"How long have you known her?" Axel asks.

"As long as I've known her husband. About five years now."

"I think what they're not saying is from the outside looking in, things aren't as black and white as you just taking care of a friend's pregnant wife," Detective Greer says.

He's been joining us more and more since he's become a friend. Currently, he's been on the lookout for his own cabin up here in the mountains. He told us a while ago to call him by his first name, Evan.

"Evan, I made a promise. Nothing more. My word is everything, so this is me keeping my word. If any of you suggest I ever had feelings for my buddy's wife, I will end you now. I've never crossed that line." I tell them to put an end to this kind of talk.

"Funny, that's where your mind went. Maybe chew on that a bit." Cole says, smiling before they all change the subject.

I look back at the girls and at River. She fits in so well. The girls are all smiles and include her in the conversation. That's all I want is for her to fit in and not feel alone.

The fact that I want her to find it here and stay here means nothing. Right?

CHAPTER 6

RIVER

I'm lying on the couch as promised and watching Storm on his laptop, submitting some of the information needed for the benefits paperwork. I'm worried that I'm transferring my dependence of Jason onto Storm. Even though I know I relied on Jason for a lot, he leaned on me, too. So it felt balanced.

Storm has been my rock, but there is no way to help him out. So this relationship... Well, friendship doesn't feel as balanced. I don't have any option right now, so I have to make the best of it until I can get out on my own and prove I can stand on my own two feet.

Though I think things will calm down once this paperwork is done. My child and I will both receive health benefits, and there is the military life insurance. However, there is a life insurance policy Jason took out that I didn't know about until Storm found it in his desk. That's another $250,000, but that one will take just as many hoops to jump through.

Then there is all the social security paperwork. My child will receive survivor's benefits, too. This will allow me to go back to school and get an education that so I can better take care of my child.

The big question is what to go to school to study. I have months to figure it out. I won't see a penny of anything for a few months, so I've been trying to think about what I like to do and how I can turn that into a career.

"What is your birthdate, and what was your maiden name?" Storm asks as he flips through some papers beside him.

"October 5, 2000, and Phillips."

"Good news and bad news. Which do you want first?" he asks.

"Ugh, the bad news," I say, preparing for the worst.

"It can take a minimum of three months for this to go through, but can take even longer. The good news is if the baby is born before it's approved, then you will get back pay."

"That's something, at least." I sigh. Then I pull up the menu on the TV again, looking for a movie to watch. Finally, I settle on the perfect comfort movie, *Pitch Perfect*.

About twenty minutes into the movie, he closes the laptop.

"Okay. You have been doing really well. How would you like to get out of the house for dinner?" he asks.

My eyes light up. "What do you have in mind?"

"I think I'll give you a short tour of the property with a ride on the Gator, and then I know a great spot to have a picnic nearby."

"Sounds perfect," I say.

While I get ready, he packs up dinner for us. When I come back out, I meet him in the kitchen.

"You don't by chance have any cherries, do you? I just had a craving for them."

"I have some frozen ones. We can take them, and they should be good to go when we get there. Also, I have some canned fruit that has cherries in it. Take your pick."

I'm honestly shocked that he has cherries. With all these weird cravings I've been getting, surprisingly, he's had everything on hand. But so far, the cherry craving is the worst.

"Frozen, please."

He grabs a bag of frozen cherries out of the freezer and adds them to the rest of our food, and we head out.

He gives me a tour of the property. Everything from where his garden is and what is in the different outbuildings to where he has found some wild berries that would be good to pick and can for winter.

We arrive at the bank of the river and there is a fallen tree that would make a good bench and a nice patch of grass to set up a blanket for the picnic. He has the same idea because that is where he stops and starts setting up with a blanket on the ground.

Joining him, we pull out the food and arrange it on the blanket. He tells me about his way of life out here and how the other guys live. I find it absolutely fascinating being able to live off the land and do what they do. Every question I have, Storm answers.

I'm actually having a good time, and we sit and talk for long after we're done eating. We stay so long we watch the sun go down.

I have a fleeting thought that this almost feels like a date. He's so easy to talk to, and the conversation just flows. There's never any awkward silence.

But this isn't a date. My husband just died, and there's no way his best friend, who's obligated to take care of me for the next few months, wants anything more from me.

As he's talking about the group hunt he and the other guys are going to go on in a few weeks, I can't help but wonder what it would be like to kiss him. Staring at his lips, I've imagined his lips on mine so long that I don't realize that he stopped talking until he places a hand on my arm to get my attention.

"You okay? You seem like you were a million miles away," he says.

"I'm sorry! Willow calls it pregnancy brain. She says that it happened to her a lot when she was pregnant. It's really nice to know someone that's gone through all this before. I didn't have that back in Virginia." I tell him, switching gears with the conversation.

"I'm glad. A big part of you coming here was I knew you'd have the girls and the sense of community to help you out. If you ever need anything, I know that you can call anyone of the girls, or the guys, and they'll be right there to help simply because you're important to me."

The shivers that race up my spine when he says that I'm important to him have no right being there. I'm almost mad at myself for it. He's just doing a nice thing, making good on a promise he made to Jason. He doesn't mean that in any other way. I'm sure of it.

That doesn't mean my heart wants to listen.

CHAPTER 7

STORM

I was finally able to convince River to take a nap today, and once I knew she was asleep, I went outside to the barn to call my mom and stepdad. I've been texting them here and there, but I told them I would call them as soon as I was able.

"Is everything okay? I was beginning to think you weren't going to call," my mom asks. Then she switches the phone over to speakerphone so my stepdad can hear the conversation as well.

I recap what's happened over the last week since we've been back in Whiskey River, her doctor's appointments, and needing to take it easy. Then I dropped the bomb that I've been keeping from them.

"I need a favor," I say, preparing them for what's about to come next.

"Anything you need, just tell us," Mom says.

"Whatever you need, son. All you have to do is ask," my stepdad says.

"Right before we left Virginia, River was served with paperwork from Jason's parents ordering a DNA test to prove the baby was his. Jason hadn't had contact with his parents other than a few odd letters he sent to update them on what was going on. When he joined the military and married River, they disowned him. They've never replied or reached out to him. River knew all this but still sent them a letter to let them know that their son had died and that she was pregnant. But they didn't even attend the funeral."

"Did she do the DNA test?" my stepdad asks.

"Yes, she went in and took care of it. We left town early the next day and I haven't heard anything. But Jason's parents don't have my address. Actually, the only forwarding address I left was for Jack's shop in town. But he hasn't said there's been anything from them either."

"By now, they would have the results. More than likely, if anything's going to come out of this, you'll hear something in the next few weeks. But I think it's best you get her set up with a Montana driver's license and start getting her residency set here as soon as possible. Montana doesn't do well with grandparents' rights," my stepdad says.

My stepdad is a judge and a pretty high-ranking one here in the state of Montana. Before that, he was a lawyer, and he has some of the best connections that I could ask for.

When I was four, my dad died. My mom married my stepdad when I was eight. He felt it was important to sit down and talk to me about whether I wanted him to legally adopt me. When I told him my decision to keep my father's name, he was completely understanding.

Despite not being legally adopted, he's always treated me like his own son. Both he and my mom have been patient and understand that I needed space after I came out of the military. Since I was injured, I think they were just happy to have me home alive.

"I will take her down and switch everything over and get her set up here at my address. She's agreed to stay with me at least until after the baby's born, and she gets the all clear from the doctor, if not longer. I have a feeling that she's going to be pretty overwhelmed once the baby gets here," I say.

"I agree, sweetheart. Whatever you guys need, you let us know," Mom says.

"And if you hear anything from Jason's parents, you call me and let me know. I'll reach out to a couple of lawyers that handle this sort of thing and see which one can take on this case if anything were to arise," my stepdad says.

"Thank you for everything. I promise it won't be so long before I call you again."

Going inside, I peek in on River to make sure she's okay. She is sleeping peacefully with her hair spread out over her pillow. The sight of her so relaxed and sleeping catches me off guard. The way the sunlight is hitting her hair just right, and the slight flush on her cheeks makes for a beautiful picture. For the first time, I notice how absolutely stunning she is.

She looks absolutely tranquil like this. Knowing that I was able to give her a safe place, a place that she can relax and enjoy this pregnancy, does something funny to my heart.

Standing there, I watch her sleep for longer than I should. Finally, I go to the living room and sit in the recliner with one of the pregnancy books she brought with her.

I've been reading, so I know what to expect with everything that she's going through. Like the fact that morning sickness can happen throughout the entire pregnancy and not just in the morning. Now I know that her throwing up isn't as alarming as I first thought it was. But if I hadn't been reading the book, and she started throwing up, I would have panicked and dragged her to the emergency room.

It's helpful to know what she's going through, so I know the best way to help her. Things like her lower back is going to be sore. Or to make sure to watch that her ankles don't swell up, which means that she's spending too much time on her feet, and I should make sure that she sits down. That's not a problem now because the doctor has her pretty much off her feet, but something to keep in mind later on.

"What are you reading?" she giggles.

Her laughter startles me, and I look up to find her standing just in front of the hallway. Her hair is a mess from sleeping and there's a flush still on her cheeks.

She's wearing cotton shorts with some classic rock and roll band T-shirt. Even dressed so casually and just up from a nap, she looks absolutely beautiful. For a moment, I can't do anything but sit there and stare at her as the blush on her face deepens.

Finally, I remember she asked me a question, and I hold up the book and shrug my shoulders.

"I think it's a good thing to know what is going on with you and what to expect. Things like morning sickness doesn't just happen in the mornings, and learning about Braxton Hicks contractions as you move into your third trimester." I say, marking my place and setting the book down.

"Well, thank you," she says shyly.

"I was going to take the dogs back to their room and do some training with them. Would you like to join us? There's a window seat that you can sit on and enjoy the sun and watch us if you'd like."

"I'd like that," she says. Standing, she picks up the baby book I had put down and follows me back to the room.

When I let out a loud whistle, all the dogs come into the room. Though only a few come running, most of the others act like I just woke them up in the middle of the night for something.

River sits at the window seat and one of the pregnant females goes and lies on the floor beside her. Then she looks at me like she's daring me to try to pull her away.

"I guess Daisy is on guard duty and will be sitting out training today while she watches over you."

"Every night she's been in my room. When I get up in the middle of the night, she's the one that follows me to the bathroom," River says, reaching down to pet Daisy.

Seeing her love my dogs is almost the equivalent of a parent watching someone pour love and attention into their children.

I enjoy having her in the room as I work on some of the training with the dogs. It's funny how they want to show off for her. It's obvious that her presence is making the dogs do a lot better than they normally do.

When it's time for dinner, she insists on helping me because she wants to get up and stretch her legs. I know it has to happen since she's been very good at keeping off her feet all day.

As we prepare the lasagna, she has a bowl of cherries sitting on the counter that she eats every so often. She's still craving them, and we are almost out, so a trip into town to stock up will be a must in the next few days.

While we're preparing dinner and moving around the kitchen, I could almost swear she's flirting with me. Maybe if it was anybody but River, I'd flirt back. But I'm pretty sure I'm just misreading this as her being nice. We've been in each other's space constantly, and I think I'm just overreacting to things.

We work together in the kitchen really well, and I find myself looking forward to many more nights of making dinner together just like this.

"I think I want to take a bath, is that okay?" she asks after dinner, and we're done with the dishes.

"Of course it is. Why don't you use my bathroom? There's a big claw foot tub in there, and I think you'll be more comfortable," I tell her. At my words I'm fascinated with the way her eyes light up.

"I'm going to take you up on that. Thank you."

"Here, let me help you get it set up. The girls sent some fancy bath salts and oils that they thought you might like. I put them in the closet so I'll pull them out for you. Why don't you can pick what you'd like to use in your bath? "I follow her into the bathroom.

After grabbing some towels for her, I get the water running so it can warm up. Then I get the basket of items from the closet and set it on the counter for her. While I'm doing all this, she comes in with clothes that she sets on top of the towels.

Turning back to the tub, I test the water, and then plug the drain so it can start filling for her. When I turn to look at her, she's watching me. Suddenly, the bathroom feels tiny with her standing there. I know I need to get out and let her have her bath in peace.

"Well... umm... just... call me if you need anything," I say, starting to move towards the door. But I freeze when she places a hand on my arm.

"Thank you, Storm, I really appreciate it," she says, smiling.

Nodding my head, I bolt out the door, closing it behind me. I don't stop until I'm across the house, enclosing myself into the laundry room. It's then I finally take a deep breath.

I'm trying to do everything I can to not imagine her taking a bath in my bathroom. With her naked body sliding into my large claw foot tub, her hair pinned up and the bubbles on top of the water all around her. Hell, even the slight bump of her baby belly when she's standing there naked turns me on.

This is my best friend's wife. I shouldn't be this hard from just a few minutes together in the bathroom. I need to get it together because I'm sure River would be horrified to walk in and see me hard as nails from the thought of her using my bathtub.

Somehow, I get the feeling Jason is going to find a way to make me pay for this from beyond the grave.

CHAPTER 8

RIVER

I've been applying for job after job and keep getting denials or ghosted. If I have any chance of getting out of Storm's hair, then I need to get a job and start saving some money.

After sending out a few more applications and checking my email, I find another denial email. Oh, they're nice about it. At least they try to be, but it doesn't make it any less hurtful. Groaning, I rest my head on the desk, thinking how I'm probably just applying in the wrong field. Maybe I need to switch gears, but I do not really have the energy to do so right now.

"River? What's wrong?" Storm says, stepping into the office doorway.

I should just say nothing and move on, but it seems like he came in at the perfect moment where I just need to unleash on someone.

"Do you have any idea how expensive childcare costs are? So, if I'm going to be making any money at a job, I have to find one that I can work from at home. Most of those include a typing test which I seem to keep failing. But for a job that doesn't include typing, they turn out to be one of those stupid MLM sales jobs. I am not someone who can sell someone anything." I stop to take a deep breath, intending to go on.

"River, you need to stop stressing. I know all of this is a lot to think about. But as long as you're staying here, I'm going to take care of you. For as long as you need, and for as long as you want." His voice is calm and somehow reassuring.

"I know. But there is even a limit to your generosity. I don't plan on reaching that limit anytime soon, nor do I want to over-stay my welcome," I sigh, leaning back in the chair.

"There is no limit, River," he says.

The stare he's giving me tells me without words that he's serious.

"So, if I wanted to stay here until this kid turns eighteen and graduates high school, you'd let me?" I joke with him trying to prove my point, but he just stares at me as if I should know the answer is yes.

"I mean what I say. So will you please stop stressing about it?" he says gently.

I just nod my head.

"Now, let's get you out of the house for a bit."

Standing quickly, I am immediately excited to see what he has planned.

"Where are we going?"

"Well, I got a call from the animal shelter. They have a dog that they think will do well with my training. Every so often, they call me, so I thought I'd head into town and check it out. But it's also a good time to go and get your driver's license changed from Virginia to Montana."

"Oh, we don't have to do that right now. It seems like it would be such a pain to do it once I move out." I say it because I hadn't even thought about changing my driver's license.

But I also don't miss how Storm shifts on his feet uncomfortably.

"What are you not telling me?" I narrow my eyes at him.

He doesn't look up and make eye contact with me. Instead, he appears to be looking past me.

"Once we get your driver's license settled, that will start your residency in Montana. Fortunately for you, Montana doesn't look too kindly on grandparents' rights. So whatever Jason's parents have in mind with requesting that DNA test, you will have a better chance as a Montana resident than a Virginia resident."

In my heart, I can't bring myself to believe that his parents would be that horrible towards their own grandchild. But it's always better to be safe than sorry, I think to myself. Then my mind starts racing, thinking of what I need to take with me.

"Go get dressed. I already pulled all the paperwork and have it ready on the counter. Everything that we need was in with Jason's stuff, and we've been using it for the military paperwork," he says. Then he steps out of the doorway, letting me pass.

"Thank you." Without thinking about it, I once again place my hand on his arm and look up at him. Offering a small smile, I lock eyes with him.

When he nods at me, I go get dressed. I don't know how he does it, but Storm always finds a way to completely throw me off balance. The worst part is I don't know if he's doing it on purpose or if he doesn't even realize he's doing it.

Knowing I'm going to have to take a photo for my new driver's license, I put a little extra time into my hair and makeup before stepping out of my room. Storm looks up at me when I come into the living room, putting this phone away. But then does a double take, looking at me again. Normally, attention like that would make me uncomfortable, but with him it doesn't, so I just shrug my shoulders.

"Figure if I'm going to have to have my picture taken, I might as well look good."

He grabs the paperwork off the table and before I know it, we're on our way to Whiskey River.

The small little DMV in Whiskey River is nowhere near as busy as the ones I've had to deal with in Virginia. Happily, we are in and out in about an hour.

"Well, I guess it's official. I am now a Montana resident. You know I've never lived in any other state but Virginia my whole life?" I say, staring at my Montana driver's license.

It may have Storm's address on it, but it's that first sign of independence. Kind of like it was when I saw my married name after Jason and I were married.

As we pull into the parking lot of the animal shelter, I put my driver's license away. We are here for the puppy that Storm is looking at, and I'm very interested in finding out what makes a good puppy for him.

The little old ladies at the animal shelter know him as soon as he walks in, and they're all smiles. He introduces me to each of them, but again, I don't remember their names.

"River, Storm here told us about you the last time he was in. He's so excited to be an uncle to your child. We heard what happened to your husband though, and we are so sorry. We wish you were in Whiskey River for better circumstances, but we are darn glad that you're here." The taller of the ladies says before turning and leading us to the back of the building.

"This guy here seems to have some searching abilities. Not only did he track down two of our lunches this week, but when he sniffed out my medications in my purse, he sat on it and started barking," she says.

"Well, it sounds like he's definitely got some experience. What brought him to the shelter?" Storm asks.

"His owner died, and the kids didn't want to or couldn't take him."

"River, you stay out here until I know that the dog's friendly enough for you to be in with him. We don't want him jumping up on your belly." Storm tells me as he enters the room where the dog is waiting for him.

Waiting by the door, I'm able to watch the whole interaction through the windows. He's patient and gentle with the dog who takes his time, sniffing Storm out. But in just a few minutes' time, Storm is petting the dog, and they're acting like their best friends.

Storm comes out of the room with a big smile on his face. "Looks like this guy is coming home with us," he says and brings the dog to the door.

The dog looks at me, sniffs around me and then sits down and stares up at me with what I swear is a huge smile. When I lean down and pet him, he starts doing a little happy dance spinning in circles, trying to lick my hand.

We all laugh because this dog just has the most amazing energy. At one point the dog gets so excited he pushes against my leg, and I get a little off balance falling in to Storm.

I land against his hard chest, and he studies me with a hand on each arm. When I look up at his face, there's something more than just the laughter that was there a moment ago.

"Sorry," I say as I start to pull away.

"No need to be sorry. I'll always catch you," he says in his deep voice, making my heart do a weird flutter.

As we head up front for him to fill out the paperwork for the dog, I take a few deep breaths and try to get those thoughts out of my head. This is Storm, after all, not just some other random guy.

On the way home, I told Storm that I wanted to sit in the back seat with the dog.

"I don't think that's a good idea. What if he gets too excited and bumps into your belly?" Storm keeps a hand on the truck door so I can't even open it.

"I'm a lot tougher than I look. Plus, I think that it's going to be stressful in a new truck not knowing where he's going, so I can be back there to give him a little reassurance."

Storm still looks hesitant, and it's actually kind of cute.

"I'd rather you sit up front with me," he says. But not with as much determination as last time.

"Storm, I've always wanted a dog. Whenever I thought about the drive home, I knew I wanted to sit in the back. At least let me get the experience of bringing a dog home," I tell him with a smile. Then I gently place my hand over his to open the truck door. This time he lets me.

The dog jumps inside all excited and moves to the far side, giving me plenty of room to get in with him and sit down. Storm makes sure I'm buckled up before he closes the door and gets into his seat.

Carefully, the dog walks over to me, laying down, resting his head in my lap. I'm happy to just sit there petting him. On the drive up the mountain, Storm keeps checking the rearview mirror to make sure everything's okay. But neither of us moves much.

"He needs a name, you know," Storm says when we're about halfway home.

"Let's get back to the cabin and give him have some time to settle in before we name him. Give his personality a chance to shine through."

"Sounds like a plan," he says.

We do just that.

Once back at the cabin, Storm introduces him to the rest of the gang, who seemed to accept him with no questions asked. He snoops around the house and is in and out of every room at least twice before returning right back to my side.

Even through dinner, he lies beside my seat, and when I go to use the bathroom, he sits right outside the door.

"You know, I think a good name for him would be Shadow," I joke as I'm getting ready for bed.

"I think that fits him. He's pretty much been your shadow all day."

"What do you think? Do you like the name Shadow?" I turn and ask the dog. He starts wagging his tail uncontrollably.

"I think that's a yes," Storm laughs.

As I'm getting ready for bed, a few of the other dogs that have been sleeping in my room join us. But Shadow makes it clear that he is the only one laying at the foot of my bed.

"Maybe we shouldn't let him get used to sleeping in here with you. Because at some point, once the baby's born, you're going to want your space again."

"I don't know. I like having at least one dog in here if not more. It's like my own personal security team," I joke with him.

But he doesn't laugh. Instead, he studies me for a moment like he's reading what I didn't say.

"I think he knows that you're pregnant, and he's being extra protective." He steps into the room to pet Shadow, who eats up the attention. "Are you sure you're all right with him in here?"

"I'm fine with it. If I'm not, I will let you know. I promise."

That seems good enough for Storm because he turns to leave. At the same time, I move towards the bed but trip over one of the dogs. Once again, I end up falling against Storm.

This time, Storm doesn't let me go right away. Our eyes lock, and the mood definitely shifts in the air. Is it my imagination or did he just lean down a little bit? I'm trying to decide, but the next time he moves I'm certain that he did. While I'm trying to figure it out, it's clear a second later. Suddenly, his lips are on mine, and he's kissing me.

It's a soft kiss. Almost like he's asking if this is okay. I should move away and put an end to this. But I find I want him to kiss me more. So, I wrap my hand around the back of his neck and pull him in to me. That seems to be enough for him to deepen the kiss before he pulls back, putting quite a bit of space between us.

We are both trying to catch our breath while staring at each other. But we don't say a word.

After a moment, he clears his throat. "Good night, River. Get some sleep." Then he leaves the room, not letting me say a word.

Almost like he doesn't want to hear what I might have to say. Well, that makes two of us. I don't want to talk about the kiss, much less hear that in his opinion, it was a mistake.

Turning off all the lights and getting ready for bed, once again Shadow lays his head on my feet. But it seems neither of us is really going to get any sleep tonight.

CHAPTER 9

STORM

They were heading back into town for another doctor's appointment, this one just to check her vitals and make sure that everything is staying healthy. This time, a nurse that we didn't see last time takes us back to the examination room.

"Okay Mom, why don't you take this to the bathroom right here and pee? Dad can go wait in the room right over here," the nurse says.

I notice that River doesn't correct her. The word dad feels like a sucker punch to the gut. Both because it should be Jason here, but also because of how much I like the idea. The longer River is here, the more I can't wait for the child to arrive and to be part of its life, even though I never thought kids were something I wanted.

She is not carrying my kid, but I feel like an expectant father. I'm preparing for the baby to be here, and I'm taking care of her just as Jason would.

When River comes back into the room and gets settled on the exam table, I take a seat on the chair next to her.

A woman walks in that we did not see last time, and introduces herself as one of the midwives in the practice.

"I wanted to take your vitals myself just to make sure that we get them with pinpoint accuracy," the midwife says. Then she attaches the blood pressure cuff to River's arm.

"Am I going to be in the way?" I ask, ready to move the chair for her.

"Oh no, you're fine right where you are, Dad," the midwife says.

Once again River doesn't correct her. So, I reach out and take River's hand in mine. She gives it a little squeeze, as if she knows what that one word is doing to me today. Yet there's no possible way she can know.

The midwife pulls out the little Doppler and starts searching for the baby's heartbeat. Before I know it, a loud whooshing sound is filling the room again.

"There's your baby! All happy and healthy. Your vitals do look much better today, so just make sure you're taking it easy, getting plenty of rest, and try to keep stress to a minimum. We will see you at your regularly scheduled appointments," the midwife says. Then she puts the Doppler away and leaves the room.

Since we were in town, we decide to stop at Jack's store because the other guys are meeting there. But I want to make sure that she's still up for it.

"You still up for seeing everyone at Jack's store?" I ask.

"Yes, I've been looking forward to this all week," she says as we get in the truck.

Well, that seals the deal. I drive us across town and park in the back of the shop. The other guys are here today because they're selling different things that they make, but I don't have anything to sell. Mostly, I come to socialize with the guys and see what's going on.

Jack has set up a couch in the back room for the girls to sit and talk while us guys hang out around the counter in front of the store. There are a few people milling around the store. Mostly they look like tourists. They like to come in, talk, and often they get excited to meet the guys who created some of the items that they're getting ready to buy.

We've been sitting there talking for about half an hour when a single guy walks in. He starts looking around, but he's not really concentrating on anything. It's as if he's looking for something or someone. Even though we continue on our conversation, I know we all have one eye on him. None of us recognize him.

After he makes a round of the store, he comes up to the counter. "I'm looking for River. I was told she'd be here," he says. Instantly, I'm on guard, pushing my way to the front of the group.

"What can I do for you?" I ask.

"Do you know where River is?" He asks again seeming unsure. Not that I can blame the guy. He's as skinny as a toothpick, and when you've got seven mountain men standing around staring at you. It can't be a very comfortable situation.

"Depends on what you want her for. You have to get through me first," I tell him. Then I cross my arms, completely going for the intimidation factor.

"Listen, I'm just here to drop this. But I have to personally hand it to her." He holds up a manila envelope and I know instinctively that whatever is inside of it can't be good.

"River, sweetheart, can you come here a minute?" I call into the back. A moment later she emerges with a smile on her face, but when she takes one look at me, the smile drops.

"You can place the envelope in her hand, and then I suggest you leave," I say.

He does just that. The envelope barely touches her fingers before he's bolting out the door.

Not giving her a chance to worry about what is inside, I take the envelope from her and lead her back to the couch in the back. Then I sit on one of the available chairs while I open it.

The other men join me, and you could cut the tension with a knife. We all prepare ourselves to see what the papers inside say.

"It's Jason's parents, isn't it?" River asks as I pull the papers out.

Unfortunately, she's right.

"It looks like they are trying to sue you for custody. I was afraid of this when they requested the DNA test," I say.

"May I?" Jack steps up, and since he was a lawyer before he became one of us, I hand the papers to him.

"You said you took her to get her Montana driver's license earlier this week?" Jack asks.

"Yes, with my address on it."

"That was a good move, setting up her residency here in Montana. This state does not do well with grandparent's rights. Even if they could provide a better life for the child, it's always the rule to stay with the parents. As long as the parents are capable of taking care of them," Jack says.

Emelie is sitting next to River, and she wraps her arms around her, pulling her close to her side. Then the other girls circle the wagons, getting close enough to put an arm or hand on her, giving her strength.

"Jason and I talked on deployments, and he never really had much good to say about his parents. They were strict, not friendly, and they never wanted him as a kid. When he joined the military and married River, they disowned him. They didn't even go to their own son's funeral. Why the hell do they want custody of his child?"

"Do you remember anything else that Jason might have said to you about his parents?" Jack asks.

"He said that they are always spending money, but when he needed certain things, they couldn't afford it. He said he wasn't sure if they didn't have the money or they just didn't want to spend the money on him," I tell them.

"Give me their names, and I will do a little digging into them. I've still got some contacts," Phoenix says.

His parents had one of the biggest tech companies outside of California. When they died unexpectedly, it all went to Phoenix, who had no desire to run it. Though selling everything off made him billions. He's been very smart and kept a lot of contacts in the circle that he used to run in.

"With your permission, I will represent you guys here in Montana. This child isn't even born yet, so I'm not sure how they got this filed. But it should be pretty easy to throw out. With the child not even being born yet, the child's home state will be here in Montana, which will govern this trial. I'll make sure of it," Jack says.

"What can we do to help?" Willow asks.

"Help River get settled here. The more settled she is and the more that she makes this home, the stronger the case we have," Jack says.

"Well, that's the fun part. Let's talk baby showers," Sage says.

We leave the girls in the backroom and head back out to the counter to talk.

"Is there anything I need to know about River, or anything in her background that the parents might try to use against her?" Jack asks me.

"I don't know. I'd have to ask her. She was a foster kid and moved around a lot until she hit high school. The family that she was with was pretty good from what I understand. Though she doesn't talk a lot about her life before she married Jason and I never pried," I tell him.

"We'll see what you can find out. Let's make sure we don't have any surprises," Jack says.

CHAPTER 10

STORM

As soon as we walk in the door, Shadow runs right up to River, sniffing her. Then, he attaches himself to her side. Right then, I know that dog is meant to be hers and I will train him to protect her and that baby.

When she does move out, it'll be good for her to have extra security. I don't like how my gut twists when I think of her moving. But I know I have time. While this stuff is going on with Jason's parents, she won't think about moving out. So I know I have at least until the baby is born before I need to start worrying about her moving.

"I think I'm going to go lay down for a bit. Is that okay?" she asks hesitantly.

"Of course. Go lie down and get some rest. I want to take some of the dogs outside to stretch their legs and do some outside training. That way, we don't wake you," I say, watching her walk down the hallway, Shadow right at her feet.

Taking a few of the dogs outside, I toss a ball and let them run around before putting them back in to the sunroom. Then I step out to the barn to call my mom and stepdad and give them an update.

"Hey baby, how are you and River doing?" My mom answers right away.

"We've definitely been better. Is George there too? Can you put me on speaker-phone?" I want to talk to my stepdad, to make sure that they both know what is going on.

"Yes, honey, he's right here. Let me switch the phone over." Then, the background noise changes.

"Is everything all right?" My stepdad gets right to the point.

"When we were in town today, River was served with papers. Her forwarding address was a buddy's shop in town. We were there visiting when she was served."

Then I read them the paperwork that we were given.

"I was afraid that it was going to be something on this based on the court ordered DNA test," my stepdad says.

"But this can't stand, can it? She hasn't even had the baby. They can't try to take it from her," Mom says, getting all worked up almost as if it was her own grandchild that was being threatened.

"I'm glad you got her license changed to Montana. With how little rights grandparents hold in the state, I'm not sure how they got a legit lawyer to even take on this case," my stepdad says.

I can picture him rubbing the bridge of his nose like he does when he gets annoyed.

"My buddy Jack used to be a really good lawyer, and he said he's going to look into all this," I tell them, hoping to calm their fears.

"What do you mean, used to be a lawyer?" my stepdad asks.

"He was really good at what he did, but the law office that he worked with made him defend criminals. When he had to defend people that admitted to him that they were guilty of horrible crimes, it weighed hard on him. Eventually, it pushed him over the edge, so he stopped practicing. After moving here, he opened an outdoor store and does pro bono work for charities in the area, particularly the women's shelter. He's helped some of the other guys out too, as needed."

When my stepdad asked for Jacks' name and information to look him up, I give it to him.

"Now, what do you know about Jason's parents?" My stepdad is completely in lawyer mode, getting all the information needed.

In a way, it's comforting to take the emotion out of it and stick to the facts right now.

"All I know is what Jason has told me over the years. He and River were really good friends and towards the end of high school, it became more. He decided to join the military. When he finished boot camp, he and River were married. Though his parents never approved of the military or River, and disowned him when they got married. He sent them a few letters with updates over the years, but never heard a word back.

What started all this is River sent them a letter letting them know about Jason's death and that they were going to be grandparents.

"She did nothing wrong by contacting them. In fact, it would have seemed odd if she didn't. But that this is their first conclusion, to try to take a child from a marriage they didn't even want to happen, just doesn't sit well with me. What about River? What do you know about her?"

"I've known her just as long as I've known Jason. They were married when we met. She was a foster kid, has no family, and bounced around from house to house until she found a somewhat steady place when she was in high school. But it's why Jason asked me to watch over her. He knew if anything were to happen to him, she didn't have anyone. At all the Unit's events, River would help out, and she was always the first one to volunteer when someone needed help. She was very involved with the other military wives. But I don't know anything of her childhood. I never pried, as it wasn't my place."

"I understand. If she was a ward of the state, we should be able to get her file pretty easily."

"There's more than what you're telling us, "Mm says after being silent for so long. It's not an upset voice. Just that curious mom tone of wanting to find out what I'm holding back.

I don't know what to say because I hadn't planned to admit anything to my mom.

Much less say the words of what I'm feeling out loud.

"I can hear it in your voice when you speak. There's something else there," Mom says gently. I don't keep secrets from my mom. I never have, and she knows that if she just keeps pushing long enough, I will break and tell her.

"It's absolutely the worst timing, and I don't even know what to do about it. But I'm starting to have feelings for her. While, I know how wrong it is and how much of a horrible friend it makes me, but with her living here, I don't know how to stop it."

"It doesn't make you a horrible friend. It makes you human. You're both bonding over a very traumatic event, and that's completely normal. Just be careful with your emotions and hers," Mom says. "You should bring her for dinner, as we'd like to officially meet her."

"I'll see what I can do. It'll be all up to how she's feeling."

We talk for a little longer, catching up on what's going on with them before I hang up and head back into the cabin. When I walk in through the sunroom where all the dogs are, they seem tense and on edge. Now I'm on full alert as I step into the main part of the cabin.

Moving down the hallway to check on the River, that's when I hear it. Even though her bedroom door is closed, I can still hear her crying through it. The sound of her weeping breaks my heart.

I stop in front of her bedroom door, which is cracked open. She is lying in bed with tears pouring down her face. I guess I should have known that the events of today would catch up with her.

Shadow is lying on her feet, but he looks at me like he's not sure what to do. Without even thinking about it, I slip off my shoes, climb into bed, and pull her into my arms.

"We're going to fight this together. And remember you're not alone anymore. You've got friends here," I say, holding her tighter.

"I don't know what I'm going to do. I can't afford to pay Jack right now. Plus, they're your friends, and they're just being nice to me," she sobs.

"Jack isn't going to charge you anything. That's just how he rolls. Any other expenses that come with this, I am covering. Also, I can promise you they're your friends too. Those girls have accepted you as one of their own. There's no going back." I place a kiss on the top of her head.

After holding her for a few minutes, she seems to calm down, so I tell her about the conversation I had with my mom and stepdad.

"Mom invited you to dinner. She wants to meet you."

"Your parents aren't going to like me. Better to just put it off as long as you can," she sighs, defeated.

"Where is that even coming from? My parents are going to love you." I reassure her.

"Jason's parents hated me from day one. Never really had anyone's parents like me," she says.

Now that she's done crying, I can clearly hear how tired she is.

"My parents are different. You just wait and see. They can't wait to meet you."

"Okay, I'll take your word for it," she says doubtfully.

Neither one of us moves, and after a while her breathing evens out. Even though I can tell she's asleep, I just sit there and hold her. I really like having her in my arms and am not ready to let go of her just yet.

Kissing the top of her head, I make another promise that I'm going to take care of her no matter what. Then the sun sifts through the window and the wedding photo of her and Jason on her dresser catches my eye.

Jason, I hope you can forgive me for all this one day.

CHAPTER 11

RIVER

Today we are driving into Bozeman to have a late lunch or early dinner with Storm's parents. The closer we get to the city, the more my nerves seem to kick in.

Storm has been trying to keep my mind off of it by telling me different stories from his childhood. But the further we get away from Whiskey River, the less relaxed I feel.

"Hey, are you okay?" Storm reaches out, placing a hand on my arm to get my attention.

"Sorry, I didn't realize coming back into a city would make me so anxious. I got used to being up in the mountains, I guess." He deserves at least to know what is on my mind.

Glancing over at me, he slides his hand down from where it was on my arm and takes my hand, lacing our fingers together, giving it a squeeze. It's a fairly intimate gesture, but surprisingly, it calms me down.

Things have shifted between us since the other night when he crawled into my bed, holding me while I cried. After I didn't have one more tear left, I must have cried myself to sleep. But then he held me all night. The last time I felt that safe was when I was in Jason's arms, right before we found out about his last deployment.

Not too much later, we enter a very nice area in Bozeman and finally get to our destination. As we pull into his parents' driveway, I take my first look at Storm's boyhood home. The house is a complete contrast to his cabin in the woods.

No sooner do my feet hit the ground than an older couple is coming out the front door towards us. The woman walks right towards me and wraps me in a big, welcoming hug.

"Oh, look at you! Aren't you just the cutest thing? Let's get inside so you can sit down and get your feet up. I remember when I was pregnant with this guy. All I wanted to do was keep my feet up because my back would hurt so much." She loops her arm through mine and steers me towards the front door.

When I look back at Storm, he and the older man who I assume is his stepfather are walking behind us both with smiles on their face. Once inside, I'm seated in a large plush loveseat, and Storm takes a seat right next to me, resting his arm on the back of the loveseat behind me. With him being this close, I have to fight the urge to rest my head on his shoulder and let go.

There's already a tray of water on the coffee table as Storm's mom and stepdad take their seats.

"I am so sorry for your loss. I remember Storm talking about Jason all the time. He seemed like such a good guy. But we're also very happy to have you here with us now," Storm's mom says, smiling sadly.

"Thank you," I say. Though I'm still very unsure of what to say when people say they're sorry for my loss. Words just don't seem to fit how I feel.

"If there is anything I can do to help you get ready for the baby or answer any questions, I am happy to. Storm, please give her my phone number," his mom says. She looks at him and gives him 'the do it now or else look,' which I think is really sweet. Obediently, he reaches into his pocket, pulls out his phone, and texts me his mom's number.

Adding it to my phone, I send her a quick text back so that she has my number. When she checks and sees that what I've done, she smiles and nods.

"Now, what do you still need to get for the baby?" she asks again.

I just shake my head because this is something I've been avoiding thinking about. "I haven't really thought about what I need. Honestly, I'm a little overwhelmed because there's just so much."

"Well, the spare bedroom across the way from yours is for the baby. We can start getting what you need and putting it in there," Storm says.

Turning, I look at him in shock. My expectation was to have the baby with me in my room. I didn't think he would give me an entire room for the baby. On top of everything, he was giving up the guest room for me.

"Don't look so shocked, sweetheart," he whispers in my ear for only me to hear.

"We find out next month if it's a boy or a girl, and we will go from there, I guess," Storm says.

"Oh, that's so exciting. It's been such a long time since I've had a reason to shop for small baby items. I'd love to take you out shopping for a girl's day. We'll get things to decorate the nursery, everything the baby will need. Also, buy some cute baby clothes. Oh, we could go get pedicures and have lunch too!" She claps her hands together with a delighted smile on her face. "

Looking at her, I don't think she could be any more excited if it was her actual biological grandkid that was being born. Though my kid isn't going to have any biological grandparents around, Storm's family will be the closest they have.

We talk all through lunch about different things for the baby. In her opinion, there were things that she thought were a waste of money and things that I shouldn't live without.

She goes on to tell me about how one of the men her husband works with just had a grandchild. How different things are now, and how much they're learning through their friends.

After lunch, we get down to business talking about the paperwork that I was served. Storm brought it up, and his stepdad reads over it. Though I'm pretty sure he already has an idea of what it says.

"I reached out to Jack and told him I was your stepdad. Also, that I was not making it very known that we were connected. But being that I was a District Court judge based out of Montana, we agreed that I'd basically be an advisor on the case. Though we would keep it to ourselves that I know anything about the case. At least for right now. It's a conflict of interest, so I need to tread carefully and give the assigned judge a chance to do things the right way. But rest assured, I will be watching this case like a hawk."

"Thank you, George," Storm says, addressing his stepdad by his name, which temporarily catches me off guard.

It's apparent that I don't know much about the relationship he has with his stepdad other than it seems to be a good one. At least from everything I've heard from Jason and that I've seen today, I agree with them.

The conversation gets lighter as we wind down. In order to make it home before nightfall, Storm and I get ready to head back to Whiskey River. His mom sends us home with enough leftovers to feed us for days. Also, she makes us promise that we will get together to go shopping once I know whether it's a boy or a girl.

Once we're in the truck and heading back towards the mountains, a sense of relief fills me.

"I told you they'd like you," Storm says, grinning.

"I have to be honest. I am shocked at how welcoming your parents were. It's not something I'm used to." I look over at him and smile.

Taking his eyes off the road for a brief second, he looks at me. Our eyes lock, and then he's back, focusing on the road. But he reaches over and takes my hand just like he did on the way here like it's a perfectly normal everyday gesture for us.

"My mom's really excited to take you shopping for the baby. Are you all right with that?"

I like that he's checking with me instead of just assuming.

"Honestly, your mom is the closest thing this baby's going to have to a grandparent. Not to mention the closest thing I'm going to have for any kind of motherly advice during this pregnancy. So, yes, I'm ecstatic that she wants to be involved being that it's not her grandbaby."

"You will be important to her because you're important to me. That's how my family works."

"Well, I'm just not used to that. It will take some time to get used to it."

"We have plenty of time. I told you there is no rush for you to go anywhere," he says as his thumb makes slow lazy circles on my hand.

It's such a small and simple movement, but it has me so damn turned on that I shift in my seat to relieve the pressure. Only it doesn't work, it causes movement on the sensitive parts of me, and I have to bite back a gasp. I try to shift back to the position I was in before, but again that motion just seems to amp things up.

"You okay?" he asks, pulling my attention off my current situation.

"Yeah, I'm fine." I try to blow it off, but he doesn't seem to buy it.

"Come on. Something is bothering you. Tell me what it is so I can help you figure it out."

Obviously, he's completely unaware that would be crossing a line we have yet to cross and one I'm not sure I want to.

But he looks over at me with that face I'm sure I can trust, and knowing he is the one person on my side no matter what right now, I'm not able to keep my mouth shut. It's as if my mouth has a mind of its own, so I clamp it shut and just shake my head.

"Come on. No secrets, River. We have been through too much recently for that."

"It's the hormones. I don't think I've ever been this horny in my life," I blurt out. Then

I slap my free hand over my mouth because I can't believe I just said that out loud.

He's quiet, but I get brave enough to look over at him, and his eyes are on the road as we climb the mountain to his cabin. But his breathing is heavy, and the grip he has on my hand has tightened.

"Do you... need some help... to get... relief," he asks.

He's choosing his words carefully, and knowing Storm, he probably is.

"No, I can do it myself," I say, barely above a whisper. Then drop my eyes to the dashboard in front of me.

Until we pull into the driveway and park in front of his cabin, we are silent. Getting out, we walk into the living room as if nothing is wrong. Yet the moment the lights are on, and we look at each other again, there's awkwardness between us.

"Have a good night, River," he says, his voice rough and scratchy.

Expecting him to let me run off to bed and end the awkwardness, I'm shocked when instead he pulls me in for a kiss. A gentle kiss, but one that still ramps up everything I am feeling down there. Making the need worse with a few gentle strokes of his tongue, ensuring I will be thinking of him tonight.

When he pulls back, I'm a little dazed. But I don't wait for him to speak again. I just turn and walk to my room. It's going to be a long night. Now I need to figure out what box has my vibrator in it.

CHAPTER 12

STORM

Standing there, I watch her scurry off to her room. It's way too early for bed, but she seems determined to go, and I'm pretty sure I know why. I take a few of the dogs, head out to the barn, and do some repairs I've been putting off. Right now, It's better to not even be in the same building.

The thought of her getting off is too much. Just her words in the car had me hard as nails. I was trying to control myself because the last thing I want to do is scare her off. But I had to kiss her goodnight. A silent plea to be the one she is thinking of when she gets orgasms.

When I check the time, it's been an hour and a half, so I wrap up and go inside. Since I've got some sawdust on me, I need to shower before getting ready for the night. As I'm heading to my room, a noise catches my attention. I stop to make sure every-thing is okay, but then it hits me that I'm hearing River's vibrator and her soft moans.

I could have lived the rest of my life and been okay not knowing that my best friend's wife sounds this sweet when she is turned on. Even though I should keep walking and go to my room showering like I planned, I don't. Instead, I walk to her door and lean against the door frame taking in every sound.

Every little intake of breath and light moan makes me want to burst in there and finish the job myself. The sounds alone have me ready to cum in my pants like a goddamn teenage boy. What is this woman doing to me?

Reaching into my pants, I grip my dick, trying not to cum. At the same time, she gasps and moans making me just give in. I start stroking myself and listen to the most erotic sounds I've ever heard in my whole life.

I can tell she is getting close, and I pray she goes over the edge soon because once she does, I can walk away and forget this ever happened. Those are my thoughts, at least until I hear her lightly moan my name.

Hearing my name, I have to bite my tongue as I start cumming in my pants. Without a doubt, I'll remember the way she just said my name for the rest of my life. That light breathy moan and the urgency in her voice will never leave me. As I regain my senses, I hear her orgasm, and it's the sweetest sound in the world.

It takes every ounce of willpower I have to walk into my room and right to my shower. The cold water does nothing to calm me down, but I try to focus on getting ready for bed. Finally, I leave the bedroom to feed the dogs and make sure the house us locked up for the night.

When I open my bedroom door, I come face to face with River in the hallway. Everything I've been trying to push out my head coming flooding in. Something takes over, something I've been holding back out of respect for Jason.

"I heard you little girl," I say, the alpha in me I've been holding back coming out.

She stops and looks at me with her eyes wide, but not in fear. Her nipples turn hard under her shirt, and her breathing picks up. Apparently, she likes what she is hearing. It would be so much better if she just yelled at me.

"I'm sorry," she mutters as her face turns bright red, but she doesn't run.

"Don't you dare apologize, that was sexy as fuck. I just wish it had been me giving you relief." I take a step toward her. "Maybe next time you will let me."

She says nothing, but the sharp intake of breath tells me she likes the idea. I take another step toward her until I'm only a foot away. Slowly I bring my hand up, so she has plenty of time to step back or walk away, only she doesn't move.

I run the back of my hand over her chest and down over one of her breasts. The friction on her nipple causes one of those sexy moans I heard earlier. She's not wearing a bra, and the only thing separating my hand from her chest is the thin shirt she is wearing.

When I rub my thumb over her nipple again, I am rewarded with another one of those moans. I'm already so turned on it's as if I didn't just get relief twenty minutes ago.

She reaches out and grips my shirt at my waist, and holds on for dear life. At the same time, she is pulling me closer. A glance behind her into the living room has my eyes landing on a photo of me and Jason.

I freeze. I can't do this. This isn't right.

"Go to bed, River, before we do something we can't take back, and you will regret it." I take a big step back away from her, my eyes still locked on the photo of Jason.

She hesitates for a minute, then goes to her room, but pauses in the doorway.

"I wouldn't regret it, Storm," she says, walking into her room.

"Lock your door, River," I call through the now closed door, and I don't move until I hear the lock click.

Only then do I check on the dogs and head back to my room. I should lock my door to prevent her from coming into my room, but part of me craves her being in here. There is no way I will keep her from me if that is what she truly wants or needs.

After getting into bed, I don't bother trying to sleep. I pull out my cock that is rock hard again and in desperate need of relief. Then I start play in my mind what would have happened if I hadn't stopped us.

I'd have allowed her to pull me into her, and then I'd have kissed her. Then I'd tug her against me, letting her feel how hard I am. Right there in the hallway, I'd back her up against the wall and grind into her just to hear another one of those gasps.

Then I'd reach up and find out what she had on under that large shirt. My guess is nothing but a pair of panties. It would have been so easy to pull them to the side and have complete access to her. Complete freedom to find her clit and rub it, getting her all worked up again.

It wouldn't matter that she had just given herself some relief. I'd have her dripping and in need all over again until she was begging for me. Then I'd pull my cock out and slam it home.

Just the thought of being inside her is what sets me over the edge and has me cumming all over my bed.

This girl is going to take me to the edge of my sanity, and I can't wait for the ride.

CHAPTER 13

RIVER

Today we are having dinner at Jenna and Phoenix's place. Jack and his wife are joining us. There have been some discoveries in my case to go over.

Tomorrow, we find out if the baby is a boy or a girl. The last few weeks have been filled with flirting, chaste kisses, and a lot of teasing trying to make the other one break. I love the little games we play at home. Even now, across the room from each other, his eyes are on me.

As we help Jenna finish up dinner, us girls are catching up. They are asking about my pregnancy and wanting to know how I'm doing. It's great to have some girl time, yet I can feel the intensity of Storm's eyes on me. When I look over at him, and our eyes lock, I wink. Me being a little flirty makes him shift in his seat. Though, I can see the irritation on his face that he has to keep his distance.

Once dinner is ready, we all sit down at the table. The reason we are here comes out. Storm is sitting next to me as Jack brings up the case.

"Phoenix has found out a few things about Jason's parents," Jack gets the ball rolling.

"Now, this can't be used in court because it wasn't exactly found via legal sources." Phoenix looks at me and Storm. We both nod in understanding. "It looks like Jason's parents are in a lot of debt, and it's very possible this is a money grab."

"How is it a money grab? How can they afford an attorney?" The questions swirling in my brain come right out, and Storm rests a hand on my upper thigh under the table.

The gestures calm me and my racing mind. Well, at least until he leans over to whisper in my ear, "It's okay, sweetheart, I got you. We fight together."

Simple words with a basic meaning to anyone who might hear them, but words that mean so much more after the last few weeks.

"Well, if they get custody of the kid, they could have you paying them child support. Not only that, but they will get the social security benefits and would be entitled to up to half of the money you are getting from the military for Jason's death. As for the attorney, he owes them a favor, so they aren't even paying him. It's more like they are blackmailing him into representing this case," Phoenix says.

"They are also playing up the sob story on social media. But other than a few close friends, it doesn't look like it's getting the traction they thought it would," Jack continues.

That makes me feel a bit better. At least other people are seeing through their bullshit too.

"They were shocked you got a lawyer so fast and didn't hide the fact that they didn't think you'd be able to hire one. " Jack says. "Also, they know you are waiting on the money from the military and were trying to rush all this so you wouldn't have access to it to pay for a lawyer. I informed them I wasn't worried about money because we are counter suing them for attorney fees. I figure hit them where it hurts. With your permission, whatever fees they are required to pay I will donate to the women's shelter," Jack finishes.

"Yes, of course. You should be compensated for your time. You need to make sure you pay yourself!" I tell Jack, who is already shaking his head.

"He won't take a penny for this because he doesn't need the money. When he shares his story, you will understand," Storm whispers in my ear. Then he kisses the side of my head before turning back to the food in front of him.

The gesture doesn't go unnoticed by everyone at the table, but thankfully no one comments on it.

"Due to them wanting this settled before the baby is born and wanting it done before you get access to the large chunk of money, they are moving fast. Their object is to get their hands on the money before you have an opportunity to fight. They will try to prove you are an unfit mother, with no place to live, no job, no family, and no support system," Jack says.

Storm squeezes my thigh like a reminder that he's there for me.

"I can get my own place, and I am looking for a job," I say. At the same time, I'm trying to figure out how we disprove those claims.

"No, it will make it worse if you move again in such a short time. It could show you are unstable. Stay with Storm until all this is settled because it proves you have a support system. He will be your support in the eyes of the court and in real life. You will need it."

"My family has taken her in as part of the family. They are treating this child like it's their first grandbaby," Storm tells the group. Then he turns to me, "Plus, you have all of us here to support you. It's a much bigger support system than they have."

"He's right. All of us have agreed to show up in court to show our backing of you," Jenna says.

"Now, Jason's parents will try to throw anything and everything at you. Though, I don't see anything that they really can use unless there is anything you are holding back from us?" Jack asks.

It's a question I know he needs answered, but it also feels a bit like he's asking to protect Storm and the rest of the guys. I can't blame him. Since I'm the new girl to the group and here I am already causing a huge storm of trouble, it's hard to believe they seriously want to keep me around.

"No, I've told you guys everything. I was in and out of foster care, and I just tried to keep my head down. Early on, I learned it was easier to be invisible in a foster home and slip under the radar than to cause problems. Not all foster parents were meant to be foster parents." I shrug my shoulders like it's no big deal.

Jason knew how some nights those things that I saw happen to the other kids still haunt me. That's why he was so adamant about protecting me, and he did a great job at it.

"And what did Jason tell you about his parents? About why they weren't in the picture?" Jack asks.

"We've covered this before..." I say, getting a bit annoyed, and Storm's hand on my thigh squeezes again.

"I know, I just want to make sure we're not missing anything," Jack says.

I've seen enough shows to know that means he's trying to make sure I tell him the same story again. He wants to know I'm not lying.

"Before I entered the picture, to the outside world, they looked like a big happy family. But before I ever met them, Jason would tell me that he felt like he was more there for a photo op than to be with his parents. They tried to control every aspect of his life, and when he introduced me to his parents, it was like something snapped with them. They tried to forbid him from hanging out with me, which didn't work. He realized then that he didn't want the life they had planned. So when he turned eighteen, he signed up for the military, and they couldn't stop him. Instead of coming to terms with it, they threatened to disown him. When he married me, they followed through with that threat. I know he tried to reestablish the connection and would send them letters with updates every so often, but they would get returned without having been opened."

"Do you still have them?" Jack asks.

"They were in his office..." I say, looking over at Storm for confirmation.

"I saw them, and I kept them. They're in a box. Right now, they're sitting in my office back at the cabin," he says.

"Good. Keep them so we can show that they chose to have no relationship. That will go a long way to prove that they don't know you," Jack says.

"All right, enough of the serious talk. I made dessert," Jenna says.

Just like that, the lunch goes from serious and business to fun and friends. Storm doesn't leave my side from then on. He is constantly finding little ways to touch me as if he's just trying to remind me he's there for me.

CHAPTER 14

STORM

River and I are sitting in the waiting room at the doctor's office. Today is the day that we'll find out if the baby is a boy or a girl. Pretty much everyone in our lives has an opinion one way or another, with it being a girl having slightly more votes.

We decided that we would call and tell my parents on the way home today. Later this week, we would do something a little special for our friends in order to tell them all at once.

"Alright, River, we're ready for you. Come on back with me," a nurse says, coming into the waiting room.

We both stand and follow her back.

"Dad, you can wait and here while she goes and pees in a cup," the nurse points to the room we will be in as she hands River a cup.

Neither one of us corrects the nurse. Things have definitely shifted between River and me. I'm so excited about this little baby to get here and I feel like I have the nerves of the first-time dad if that counts for anything.

River joins me again a few minutes later sitting on the exam table. Though she looks a little nervous. Standing up, I walk over and stand in front of her resting my hands on her hips. Her hands instinctively go to my arms and that connection calms the both of us.

Not saying anything, we stand there soaking up each other's comfort until the doctor walks in. Only then do I step away and go sit back down so I'm not in the way.

"Okay, Mom, let's just get a few measurements and make sure that you're doing well. Then we'll send you down to the ultrasound to make sure the baby is doing all right," the doctor says. Then she has River lay on her back to measure her belly.

"Everything seems to be right on track. Any concerns?" The doctor asks as she feels around River's belly.

"Her vitals were up because she was stressed when we first got here. How are they now?" I want to make sure we don't miss anything.

"They're actually perfect. You would never know she had the elevation that she did a few weeks ago. Whatever you are doing, keep it up." The doctor smiles at River. When we look at each other, our eyes lock.

"Well, doctor's orders..." I say.

River starts giggling, and that beautiful sound filling the room.

"A nurse will be in shortly to walk you down for your ultrasound," the doctor says, leaving the room.

Standing, I resume my earlier position in front of River. Only this time, she playfully wraps her legs around my waist and pulls me into her. I lean down and place a quick kiss on her lips.

"Storm!" she gasps, giggling.

"Like you said, doctor's orders." I lean in for another kiss. This one starts to get out of hand. Thankfully, we're interrupted by a knock at the door right before the nurse comes in.

She takes one look at us, and a big smile fills her face.

"Right this way. Let's go get a picture of your little one," the nurse says, heading down the hallway.

I help River from the exam table and we walk behind the nurse hand in hand. She stops in front of another room filled with monitors. The lights are dim and there looks to be a makeshift bed with a chair beside it.

"Go ahead and climb on up there. Try to lie down and get comfortable. The ultrasound tech will be just a moment," she says, closing the door.

River climbs up on the bed with the same crinkly paper as the exam tables and lies down. When I sit in the chair beside her, I take her hand in mine, and we stare at each other knowing what a life-changing moment this is.

"Last chance to change your prediction and come to the majority side." I joke with her.

She's completely convinced that the baby is going to be a boy while I joined everyone else in thinking it's going to be a girl.

"Nope, because I'm sure I'm right," she smiles at me.

I don't get to reply because the ultrasound tech walks in.

"Hello, Mom and Dad. I'm Lynn. Are you ready to see your little one?" She has a big smile on her face as she sits in front of the monitor and starts hitting some buttons.

Pulling up River's shirt to expose her belly, she takes the band on her maternity pants down. Seeing her belly through clothes is one thing, but seeing the bump up close is something completely different. The pride and protectiveness that I've always felt for her multiplies.

"Alright, we're just going to put a little gel on your belly and we're going to get the first looks at your baby," Lynn says. Then she squirts some gel and uses a wand to start scanning around.

An image pulls up on the screen, and a moment later, you can clearly see the side profile of a little baby. The head, arms, and legs are all distinguishable and both of our eyes are glued to the screen. Neither of us moves until she presses a button, and the sound of the baby's heartbeat fills the room.

A vice grips around my heart and love for this little unborn human fills my chest. It's so powerful that it leaves me breathless.

"Let's see if your little one will share with us today if it's he or she," the tech says, moving the wand around. It's almost like the baby is playing a game. Every time she would get into one position, the baby would move.

"Well, she is being very playful today," the tech says, smiling. But a moment later she freezes the frame on the screen. "There we go. It looks like you're having a little boy."

"A boy," River smiles.

Turns out she has been right all long.

When she looks at me, there are tears in her eyes, but her smile keeps growing bigger. She reaches up and wipes away tears I didn't even realize were on my face. I lean into her hand. The warmth of her touch is exactly what I need right now.

Without hesitation, I lean forward and kiss her. Trying to put all the words I can't seem to say into that kiss. This moment is pivotal, and I am honored to be a part of it.

"I'm going to take such good care of both of you," I whisper against her lips and then kiss her again.

It's then I realized how hard I truly gone I am for River. Without a doubt, I'm falling for this remarkable woman. I've tried to stop myself and have tried to hold back.

From the moment she moved in with me, my fate was sealed.

It should be Jason here experiencing this moment, enjoying the pure joy on River's face. It should be him kissing her and promising to take care of them. Instead, I'm here. I have to push aside the guilt of that and focus on making this day amazing for her. Because the last thing I want is for her to be sad.

I want her to look back on the day that she found out she was having a son and be thrilled about the events that transpired. I want her to only have good memories about today.

The tech prints out multiple pictures and copies of several of them and hands them to us on our way out.

"We should call your parents and let them know," River says, taking my hand once we're in the car.

I pull her hand up to my mouth and gently kiss it, locking eyes with her. Then I dial my parent's number on the Bluetooth of my truck.

"I have been waiting for this call all day. So tell me, was I right?" My mom answers without even a hello. The pure enthusiasm in her voice is absolutely genuine, and River's smile lights up her whole face.

"We were right! It's a boy," River says.

My mom squeals loudly over the Bluetooth. "A mother's instinct always knows best," she says.

Both she and my stepdad congratulate River.

"Now that we know what we're having, we need to plan a shopping trip," Mom says.

"You let me know when, and I'll bring her into town. You two can spend the day shopping. If George isn't busy, maybe he and I can go fishing."

"I'm going to take you up on that offer. Let me know the date, and I will make sure that I am off," George says in the background.

Fishing has always been our thing.

"I don't know if Jack has said anything, but we talked, and your mother and I will be in the back of the courtroom when you are there. Please act like we aren't, as we don't want to draw attention to me being there right away," he adds.

"Okay, though I really appreciate you guys being there for us."

"That's what family is for sweetie," my mom says as we wrap up the conversation.

Once back at the house, River goes inside while I take the dogs out. When I return, I find her at the computer in the office looking up baby nursery ideas. Walking up behind her, I nuzzle my face into her neck while placing my hands on her belly.

"I can't stop thinking of all the things I can't wait to teach him, all the things I can't wait to do with him. Camping trips. Every year, the three of us going up to the lake. Teaching him how to hunt and fish, baseball or football games or whatever sport he is into." I tell her what has been on my mind.

She stops what she's doing and looks up at me with awe on her face.

"You really are excited for this baby to get here, aren't you?" she asks almost unbelieving.

"If I've given you the impression that I'm not, I'm truly sorry."

"No, I guess that was always just in the back of my head that maybe you were putting on a front out of duty."

Something about her words snaps something inside me. Taking her hand, I help her up and lead her back to my bedroom. When I set her on the bed, she looks up at me with so many questions in her eyes.

"I don't ever want you thinking anything I do with you is out of duty. I like to think we were friends at first and even if I hadn't made that promise to Jason, I would have been there for you. No matter what, I'd still be here to help you. Though now it's so much more."

Falling to my knees in front of her, I take my time removing her shoes and socks. Then I gently rub each of her feet before I stand up, sliding off my shoes, as I lean over and kiss her.

River's eyes are wide and filled with emotion as I pull away from the kiss. I can see what I hope is love and trust in her eyes, and I know that I have to be careful with her heart. She's been through so much already, and the last thing I want to do is hurt her.

"Even though I know we've been taking things slow, I want you to know that I'm falling for you, River," I say, my voice barely above a whisper. "I want to be here for you and your son. I want to build a life with you."

River's face lights up with a smile, and she leans forward to kiss me again. This time, the kiss is more urgent. The passion between us is building with each passing second. I wrap my arms around her, pulling her close, and I can feel her heart beating against my chest.

It's like that confession alone is what destroys another wall between us. Enjoying the moment, I unbutton her blouse, revealing her lacy bra underneath. My mouth begins to water at the sight of her perky breasts straining against the delicate fabric.

Moving the cup of the bra to the side, I take one of her nipples into my mouth, sucking and nibbling gently. Her breath hitches as she moans softly.

I move my attention to her other breast, exploring her soft skin with my tongue and lips before removing her bra completely. Then I pull my shirt over my head, and her hand goes to my chest.

The work I do on the property keeps my muscles well defined. She traces them and her touch drives me wild.

River then slides her hands down my chest to my waist, unbuttoning my jeans and pushing them down my legs. She looks up at me with so much tenderness, I can't help the feelings that engulf me while I enjoy her touch on me.

Taking a moment to admire her loveliness, I look at her beautiful face. Then I lean down and kiss her neck, running my hands over her body. She wraps her legs around my waist, and I lift her up. She gasps as I move her to the bed and lay her down, removing her pants and underwear.

As she lies there naked, I'm captivated by her gorgeous body and want to capture this memory. Finally, I pull away, reaching into the drawer, and get a condom. I quickly put it on before lying down next to her.

I climb over her carefully, putting none of my weight on her belly. She wraps her legs around my waist, and I slowly sink into her for the first time. We both let out a gasp, and I lean down, kissing her lightly as we both adjust to this new sensation.

Slowly, I slide in until she takes all of me. Then I have to take a moment to regain control because she feels so damn good.

My pace gains momentum as each thrust of my hips drives into her. When we move together as one, our pleasure intensifies. In the heat of the moment, our mouths find each other's.

As I build up speed, I can feel her muscles tighten around me as she cries out in pleasure. Reaching between us, I stroke her clit, knowing I won't be able to hold off my orgasm much longer. It's imperative that she cums first.

Her body starts to tremble, and her cries of pleasure fill the room as she calls out my name and her body bucks against mine. I can't help the satisfaction I feel as her orgasm ripples violently through her. Riding the sensation, I finally let go, thrusting deep inside her as I reach my own climax.

I let out a low moan and collapse onto her while being careful of her belly Once I catch my breath, I dispose of the condom and lie down next to her, pulling her close and wrapping her in my arms.

We lay there for a few moments in silence, just enjoying the moment and each other. I brush the hair away from her face and lean in to give her a gentle kiss.

I'm falling hard for this woman and I'm trying really hard not to think of the one reason I shouldn't be.

CHAPTER 15

RIVER

We planned a dinner with our friends right after we returned from his parent's house and told them we were expecting a boy. The guys were excited to have another hunting buddy added to the mix, and the girls were excited to start shopping and getting us set up with all things boy related.

Today, we're on our way to meet up with Jack at his store and do a video conference to see if we can settle all of this out of court. Jack says he's pretty sure they want to intimidate me into settling so they don't have to go to court. Since we have the law on our side, Jack says we want to go to court. Storm and the other guys trust him, so I do as well.

We get settled on the video call and exchange some pleasantries. For the first time, I get to see Jason's parents in something other than his high school graduation photo. They've aged, and they have not aged well. Part of me wants to hope that it was losing a son which did this to them, but I doubt if they cared at all. If they had, they would have been at the funeral.

"Hey, Mrs. Owens, let's get started. From what we understand, you have no family support. Is that true?" the other lawyer asks.

"Biological family by blood, no, but she does have a family here, including Storm and his parents, who are willing to stand by her," Jack answers for me.

Taking a deep breath, I try to steady my nerves. The last thing I want is for them to see me as weak. "That's correct," I say, trying to sound confident. "I may not have blood family, but I have a support system who is ready and willing to help me through this."

The other lawyers make some notes before answering their next question.

"And is it true that you don't have a job?"

"I currently do not," I answer just as Jack told me to.

So far, all the questions are exactly what Jack expected them to ask me.

The other lawyer raised an eyebrow and leaned in towards the camera. "So, you expect to raise a child without a stable income?"

"I have savings and am working on finding a job as we speak," I reply, keeping my voice steady.

"But until then, you'll be relying on your friend's charity," the other lawyer says condescendingly.

"It's not charity," Storm spoke up from beside me. "We're family, and we look out for each other."

The other lawyer looks skeptical, but there is a hint of frustration in their eyes. He knows they are losing ground in their argument.

"We're willing to offer you a settlement that will cover your medical bills and give you some financial support until the baby is born," Jason's mother finally speaks.

At her sudden intervention, I can feel my blood boil. "I don't want your money," I spit out.

The lawyers mute their mic once again and talk to Jason's parents, who just nod their heads before they unmute and continue their questions.

"Is it also true that you just moved in with another man after the death of your husband?" the lawyer asks.

"I moved in with a friend who I consider family to help get back on my feet."

"That's not what I asked. I asked if you moved in with another man," the lawyer is unrelenting.

"She answered your question. The gender is irrelevant," Jack replies, sounding bored.

The other lawyer narrows his eyes at Jack's response and takes a moment to compose himself before continuing. "It's not irrelevant. If it could affect the upbringing of the child, it's important," he says, his tone accusatory.

"I assure you that the living arrangement is strictly platonic and is in no way detrimental to the well-being of my child," I say firmly, holding my ground.

There is a moment of silence before Jason's father finally speaks up. "We just want what's best for our grandchild," he says, his voice softer than before.

"And ripping the child away from their mother is what you think is best for them?" I ask, careful not to reveal the gender. These people don't deserve to know.

The lawyers nod, scribble down some notes, and mute the camera for a moment while they talk. Jack mutes the mic, too.

"Let's take a couple of deep breaths. They aren't taking your child from you, but we need this to go a little longer. If we can get them to tip their hand, I'll know more," Jack says.

I do as he suggested, nodding my head and taking a deep breath.

"This friend that you're living with is prior military, is he not?" the lawyer asks.

"Yes, he is," I simply answered the question, but I want to be sarcastic and say obviously he is since he and my husband met while they were serving together.

One of the lawyers continues, "He has since been discharged. And we know he doesn't have a job either. After everything he's gone through, it's safe to say he probably has PTSD. Are you telling me that you find that it's a safe environment for your baby? We looked into your parent's past as well and the druggies that they are. You were exposed to the drug culture as a child. Have you turned to drugs to manage your husband's death?"

Then the other lawyer starts rapidly firing questions at me, not giving me time to answer.

My heart is racing as I listen to the barrage of questions. Even though I'm trying to stay calm, my hands are shaking with rage. How dare he insinuate that I am unfit to raise my own child?

"If you're going to ask questions and you're not going to give her a chance to answer, then we're done here. Making accusations is uncalled for. At this point, it's obvious you're reaching, so we will see you in court. There will be no further questions." Jack says coolly and calmly. The other lawyer looks startled as Jack closes the video conference.

"Why did you do that? I could have easily answered those questions. None of it's true, right?" I look over at Storm to confirm, but Jack answers.

"They wanted you to slip up. That's why they started rapid firing questions at you. One answer to one question could spin whatever narrative that they wanted. But in short, they tipped their hand and laid their cards out, so we know how to fight them now."

I stop and think about the questions that were asked.

"We already knew they were going to try to pin me as an unfit mother," I say, trying to follow his train of thought.

"And they'll keep trying to do so," Jack replies, his tone serious. "But we're prepared for them now. We know their game plan, and I'll be ready for whatever they throw at us in court."

Storm nods in agreement, his expression grim. "They don't stand a chance against us. We have the truth on our side."

Taking a deep breath, I try to calm my racing heart. It's going to be a tough road ahead, but I know that with Storm, Jack, and his parents by my side, I can face anything.

"By bringing up your parent's past, they're trying to say that you're following in their footsteps. It won't fly in court. We can easily prove with testing and medical records that Storm doesn't have PTSD. He doesn't have a job because he works for himself, and that can also easily be confirmed. But they don't need to know that. So we just allow them to think that they're on to something and continue down that path." Jack continues, seeming to understand I need a bit more reassurance.

When Jack starts shooting off an email, I sit there stunned.

"This isn't going to be a hard fight, just an entertaining one, sweetheart," Storm says for the first time, reaching for my hand.

Jack's phone rings, and he takes it, stepping outside for a moment. He comes back with a smile on his face.

"It always helps to have connections. Our court date is set for two weeks from now. I'd like to do a mock trial to get you prepared."

"My stepdad suggested the same thing. Why don't we meet at my place in a few days? We can have some of the other people there as an audience. It never hurts to have a few heads to put together," Storm says.

"I agree," Jack says.

As they discuss the details, I can't help but feel grateful for the support system around me. I never would have made it this far without them. But as the reality of the upcoming court date sets in, fear and anxiety creep in.

"What if we lose? What if they take my child away from me?" I ask, my voice barely above a whisper.

"We won't lose," Jack says firmly. "We have a strong case, and the evidence is on our side. Plus, we have witnesses who can testify to your abilities as a mother."

Storm nods in agreement. "We've got your back, and we'll fight tooth and nail to make sure that your child stays with you."

My nerves are all over the place, so once again, I breathe deeply, trying to calm myself. I know that they're right, but the thought of losing my child is too much to bear.

"Let's take a break for now. We can regroup later and discuss our plan of attack," Jack suggests.

I nod in agreement. I've had enough for today.

Storm helps me back to his truck, and we head home.

As we drive, I can't stop thinking about the upcoming court date. Closing my eyes, I try to imagine what it would be like if I were to lose my child. The thought alone is too much to even consider. I start to feel my emotions getting the best of me, but Storm's gentle hand on mine brings me back to reality.

"Hey," he says softly, reaching for my hand and holding it tight. "It's going to be okay."

"I know," I reply, my voice shaky.

Even as we arrive home, I can't shake off the feeling of anxiety. I know that my friends have my back, but the thought of losing my child is a constant fear.

Storm notices my state of mind and pulls me in for a hug as we enter the house. "I know it's scary, but we'll get through this," he reassures me.

I nod, still feeling unsure. Sitting on the couch, I can feel all the emotions that have been building up for the past few weeks overwhelm me. The tears start to flow, and I can't stop my sobs as Storm pulls me back into his arms and holds me tight.

"It's okay to cry. Let it out," he says gently.

I cry for what feels like hours until no more tears are left to shed. Storm stays by my side the entire time, comforting me and sticking right by me. As I finally start to calm down, I look up at him with gratitude.

"Thank you for being here for me."

"There is nowhere else I'd rather be, sweetheart." He kisses the top of my head as we sit on the couch, lost in our own thoughts. I am grateful that he's letting me borrow some of his strength, which I desperately need for the road ahead.

CHAPTER 16

STORM

Once River was finally all cried out, I got her to eat a little bit of dinner before helping her to bed. When I lied down next to her, she snuggled right up to me. I love this part of the night where I can have her in my arms. Sleep isn't coming easy for her, and I can tell her mind is racing.

"Jason knew who his family was," I tell her, hoping to calm her thoughts.

"What do you mean?"

"Jason had no illusions as to what kind of people his parents were. He knew they weren't good people, and it's a big part of why he asked me to help take care of you if anything happened. Even before you were pregnant, he knew they would do anything to go after the money the military would give you if he was killed in action. We talked a lot, and he knew the best place for you would be with me if anything came up."

River sniffled and buried her face in my chest. "I don't know what I would do without you, Storm."

I wrap my arms tighter around her, feeling the weight of her words settle in my chest.

"Well, you won't ever have to find out. I'm not going anywhere."

We lay there, but I can tell there is still more on her mind.

"Come on, get it all out," I say, rubbing her back.

"They came at you with PTSD..." she trails off.

It's obvious she isn't sure how to ask what she wants to know.

"You don't leave war without a few scars. It's not pretty being over there and see what we have seen. But no, I don't have PTSD. I don't like fireworks, but they aren't a trigger of any kind. I got a clean bill of health other than a limited range of motion in my right leg, which is why I was medically discharged."

River nods, seemingly relieved. "I'm sorry if I'm prying. I just worry about you."

"And I appreciate that," I say with a smile, "but there's no need to worry. I'm perfectly fine."

We lie there in silence for a few moments before she speaks up again. "Do you ever regret leaving the military?"

I hesitate before answering, thinking back to all the things that led me to my decision to retire early. "No, I don't regret it. There are things that I miss about it, but it was time for me to move on."

River nods, understanding in her eyes. "Do you ever miss the adrenaline rush or the danger?"

I chuckle lightly. "Sometimes. But nothing compares to the adrenaline rush of being with you." I nuzzle into her neck, breathing in her sweet scent.

She giggles softly, and we settle into a comfortable silence. Though a need to let her know everything will be okay fills me.

"If it came down to it, I'd submit to evaluations again. But my VA medical and discharge paperwork should be enough."

"Thank you. I hate I'm putting you through all this and depending so much on you."

I stroke River's hair soothingly. "Don't ever think that you're a burden, River. You and your child are my family now. I'll do whatever it takes to protect you both. If you had your own family, you would have moved home with them. How is this any different?"

She lifts her head to look at me with a huge smile on her face.

"Well, for one, you don't have sex with family..." she giggles.

I cut her off with a kiss before she can finish. Her lips part under mine, and her tongue darts out to meet mine. The kiss deepens, and soon we are both breathless, our bodies pressing close together. I can feel the heat from her body as she moves against me, her hands running over my chest and down to my waist.

I don't think I will ever get enough of this woman.

As our kiss intensifies, I roll River onto her back and hover over her, capturing her hands above her head with one hand while the other trails down her body. She moans softly as I trace the curves of her breasts, feeling her nipples harden under my touch. Pulling away from the kiss to look at her, I take in the sight of her flushed cheeks and parted lips, gasping for breath.

Without a word, I kiss the hollow of her neck, nipping at the skin and savoring the taste of her on my tongue. My hand continues its descent down her body until it reaches the waistband of her pants. I look up at her, silently asking for permission to continue. She nods eagerly, a hunger in her eyes that matches my own.

Slowly and with anticipation, I slide her pants down her legs along with her red, lacy panties. Her already soaked pussy is glistening, and seeing how wet she is for me turns me on even more.

Moving down her body, I press a kiss to the inside of each of her thighs. "So soft," I whisper, "and so wet for me?"

"Always for you," she moans.

"Good," I say with a smirk before running one finger along her slit. "I want to taste you."

Arousal is pulsing through my body, hardening my cock and making it difficult for me to think. I want nothing more than to bury it deep inside of her right now. But instead, I slowly lower myself until I'm face to face with her wet, pulsing core.

When I lick at her throbbing clit, she moans loudly. I love that I'm the one making her feel this way, that my touch brings her so much pleasure. Feeling even more turned on by the thought, I slip two fingers into her hot, tight pussy and work them inside of her at a steady pace. River's back arches off the mattress as I work them in and out of her.

"Oh, Storm. That feels incredible," she cries, her back still arched and hips moving in rhythm with my hand.

Then I pick up the pace, pumping my fingers into River harder as I lick her clit slowly. "Feels fucking incredible. I'm going to make you cum so hard, baby."

River moans louder as she moves against my hand. It's excruciatingly hot to watch a woman pleasured by my own hands, knowing that the sounds coming from her throat are caused by what I'm doing to her.

As she gets closer to an orgasm, she tenses and moves even faster against me. I feel her pussy tightening around my fingers as she gets closer to cumming, and it sends a surge of energy straight to my rock hard cock.

"Fuck, River. Cum on my fucking fingers," I growl as the final waves of her orgasm wash over her.

She swears and begs for me not to stop. Until the last of her orgasm has passed, I keep going with my fingers buried deep inside of her. Even when she relaxes against me, she is slow to catch her breath and is still panting. Moving up the bed, I press myself against her, making it easy for her to get used to my weight without breaking our intimate position.

I lean down to kiss her lightly while running my hands down her body. "Turn over," I instruct gently as I slip my fingers out of her pussy and lift off of her.

She turns over quickly onto her stomach, breasts pressed against the sheets and ass in the air. "Like this? Is this what you want?"

I run my hand over her pert little ass, leaning down close to whisper in a seductive voice in her ear. "Such a good girl. You're so wet and ready for me. So fucking hot."

Removing my own clothes quickly, I can feel the cool air on my cock, which makes it even harder. Ready now, I lean over River, running my hands over the curves of her ass as I press against her entrance gently.

"Tell me you want me," I command, desire racing through me.

River moans and presses back against me. "I want you so bad. Please, Storm. Don't make me wait anymore."

Moving my hips, I press the head of my cock into her entrance, slowly slipping into her tight, wet pussy. I enter her gently, savoring the tight heat around my cock as she adjusts to the size of me filling her up. When a low moan comes from River's throat, I don't resist the urge to make them grow even louder, as I push myself into her harder until I'm balls deep inside of her.

Pausing, I stop to regain some control because she feels so fucking good.

"Shit, baby," I groan.

"Move, please," she begs me insistently.

Our cries increase in volume as I thrust into her, each one punctuated by a few choice words from my lips.

"God damn, River," I whisper as we start to move together in rhythm. "You feel so fucking good around my cock, baby. So tight."

"I need more," she whimpers, and my heart swells at her words, knowing that she's enjoying this as much as I am.

Picking up the pace, I fuck her harder while holding on to both of her hips for leverage.

Firmly, I grip onto her hips, my fingers digging into her skin as I drive myself deeper and faster into her. She cries out with each thrust, her body pressing back into me, meeting each of my thrusts.

"Fuck, your pussy is begging for it. You need to cum so bad, don't you?" I growl.

"Yes. Please Storm,"

At the sound of her moaning my name, I almost cum. To gain a semblance of control, I pull out of her. She whines at the loss of my cock. Changing positions, I lie down beside her and pull her over me so she is straddling my hips and in control. My cock has a mind of its own and wastes no time getting right back inside her.

"Ride me, River," I say gruffly. "Show me what you want."

River moves her hips in a slow, sultry manner that leaves me almost breathless. She grinds herself against me in a circular motion, sending jolts of pleasure through my body with each movement.

Her breasts bounce with the motion, and her baby bump on full display only makes this even more erotic.

River leans forward and wraps her arms around my neck as she moves faster. I can feel her pussy squeeze me with each thrust, desperate for an orgasm that only I can give. Holding onto her hips, I keep a steady rhythm as she continues to ride me. She twirls her fingers through my hair, moans filling the room as we both near our climaxes.

"I'm so close, Storm. It feels so good," she whispers. "Give me more."

Her words set off a spark in my body, and I thrust up into her harder than before, feeling her tightness around me as I pound myself inside of her wet pussy. My cock twitches, and I can feel that she's close, too, her breath coming out in quick gasps as she works towards her orgasm.

"Storm," she whispers in a pleading voice. "I'm going to cum."

I'm so close, too, that I reach around and play with her clit. Her head falls back in pure ecstasy as her hair waterfalls down her back, and she pushes her breasts out. Capturing one of her nipples in my mouth, I suck hard.

A strangled cry leaves her mouth, and her body contracts tight around me as she cums hard, my name spilling from her lips. Her orgasm gives me the permission I need to let go with my own. A few seconds later, I follow with a long groan against her chest.

When I collapse against the pillow behind me, River rolls onto her side beside me. I pull her close into my arms and kiss the top of her head, feeling only contentment instead of the uneasy feeling that usually follows after sex.

Right now, the only thought running through my mind is how perfect this feels.

CHAPTER 17

RIVER

Today, we are doing the mock trial here at Storm's Cabin. Jack and his wife Sage are here, Storm's mom and stepdad, Phoenix and his wife Jenna, and Axel and his wife Emelie.

"Okay," Jack says. "These questions aren't going to be easy or nice. George here is going to act like the opposing attorney, and he's going to do everything we can think of to prove you an unfit mother. Our job today is to have you ready with a response to everything. I won't be objecting like I normally would. I will allow him to go further down the rabbit hole than I would in court. This is simply to prepare you. Ready?"

We have the dining room chairs and living room set up as best we can, like a courtroom. I am sitting at the witness stand on the kitchen island.

Taking a deep breath, I try to steady my nerves. Then, placing a hand on my belly, I think to myself, this is all for my son. I will do anything to protect him.

The room falls silent as George stands up, clearing his throat before addressing me. "Mrs. Owens, can you explain how you met your late husband?"

"We went to school together and met in class."

"During this time, is it true you lived with foster parents?"

"Yes."

"Why?"

"My parents were addicts, so I was removed from their home and placed in foster care."

"Do you have any contact with your parents now?"

"No."

"How can we be sure they won't pop into your life and drag you down the addiction path?"

"Because they are dead." I deadpan him, and he nods, taking a deep breath, looking at his notebook before starting his next line of questions.

"As a single mother, Mrs. Owens, how do you plan to provide for your child?" George asks, twisting his pen around his fingers.

"I have savings, money from the military, a life insurance policy from my husband, and I am currently looking for a job."

"So in the meantime, you are mooching off your friends. Don't you think it's unfair to burden your friends with the responsibility of supporting your child?"

"I don't see it as a burden. They are happy to offer their support and love for my child."

George scribbles something down on his notepad before looking up again. "And what about your personal life? As a single parent, how do you plan on balancing your responsibilities with the desire for companionship?"

"Right now, I am fully focused on being the best mother I can be for my son. If the right person comes along, I'll consider it, but my main priority is this child."

"Hmm, that's all well and good, but don't you think you're depriving your child of a father figure in his or her life?"

"He will have that in Storm, who can tell him all about his father. He will have that in Axel and Cole, who can't wait to show him how to hunt and live off the land. He will have that in Phoenix and Bennett, who will teach him how to protect himself, and in Cash, who will teach him to take care of others. I couldn't imagine better father figures for my child."

"Good answer, but you just revealed the gender, so be careful," Jack says.

"Here, make sure you are drinking water," Storm places some water on the counter next to me.

George continues to fire questions at me, but I respond calmly and confidently. It's not easy, but I know that this mock trial is helping me prepare for the real thing. I'll do whatever it takes to keep custody of my child.

As George finishes his questions, I breathe deeply, trying to relax my tense shoulders.

When I look at Jack, I see the concern etched on his face. "How do you think you did?" he asks me.

"I think I handled it as well as I could have," I reply with a small smile. "But it just shows how much work I still have to do."

"That's true," he admits. "But don't worry. We'll make sure you're ready for anything that comes your way."

Jack, Storm, and George take over the dining room table with notes and start talking about the case. I don't think I can take much more talk of all this, so I head over to where the girls are huddled around Jenna and her laptop.

"What are you girls doing?" I ask.

"Jenna is showing us some of the photos she took out by the river. After she edits them, she sells them in Jack's shop," Sage says, making room for me to sit and join them.

When I sit, Jenna turns her laptop towards us, revealing some of the most beautiful nature shots I've ever seen. My eyes are drawn to one in particular - another photo of the river. It's so peaceful and serene, with the sun setting behind it and casting warm, golden light across the water.

"That's amazing, Jenna," I tell her. "You have such an eye for photography."

"Thanks, River," she replies, a smile spreading across her face.

"Do you sell these online?" I ask.

"No, just prints at Jack's store," she shrugs.

"You could set up a website and offer these designs on things like canvas blankets and even sell them as stock photos. The website is super easy to set up," I say.

When I look up from the computer, all the girls are staring at me.

"What?" I ask.

"Do you know how to do all that?" Jenna asks.

"Yeah, I took computer classes in school, and I like messing around in my free time. Though I don't have a degree or anything." I brush it off.

"Do you think you can set one up for me so I can see what you're talking about? How long would that take?" Jenna asks.

"Yeah, I can do it in two or three days, depending on what is going on."

"Why don't we have a girl's night then at my place, and we can check it out and work on some of our quilts and talk baby stuff?" Emelie says.

"I'd like that. I've never been part of a girl's night before. Should I bring some food?"

"Bring whatever you are craving," Emelie smiles.

As we discuss the details of our upcoming girl's night, I feel myself relaxing. It's a welcome distraction from the stress of the mock trial and the looming custody battle. Every now and then, I can feel eyes on me, and when I look up, I find Storm watching me. Since he's already brought me more water and a snack, it's like he's making sure I don't need anything else.

Later that evening, after everyone has gone home, I find myself staring at that photo of the river again. Something about it draws me in - maybe it's the way the water seems to flow effortlessly or the warm glow of the sun as it sets behind the trees.

Grabbing a sweatshirt, I step out on the front porch, Shadow right at might side. I close my eyes and breathe deeply, letting the calmness of nature wash over me. Moments like this remind me why I'm fighting so hard for my son - so he can experience this same peace and beauty.

Storm joins me on the porch, wrapping a blanket around me.

"You, okay?" he asks, his deep voice sending shivers down my spine.

"Yeah, just needed some fresh air," I reply, leaning into him and resting my head on his shoulder as we both watch the stars twinkle in the sky.

"You're doing a great job with the mock trial," he says, rubbing my arm soothingly and holding me to his side.

"Thanks, it's just overwhelming some-times."

"I know," he replies softly. "But you're not alone in this. I'm here for you every step of the way."

I turn to look at him, his dark hair tousled by the wind, his blue eyes kind and un-derstanding. In that moment, I realize how much he means to me. I couldn't imagine going through all this alone.

"Thank you," I whisper, feeling tears prick my eyes.

"Always," he replies, his hand gentle on my cheek. Then he leans down and presses his lips to mine, a soft kiss full of tenderness and care.

I melt into him, forgetting about everything else for that moment. His arms wrap around me, holding me close as our lips move together in perfect harmony. I've never felt so safe and supported in my life, and I know in my heart that Storm is the one I want to be with. Despite our challenges, I know he'll always be there for me and my son.

As we pull away from each other, I savor the look of love in Storm's eyes. "I think we should make this a regular thing. Coming out here and enjoying some fresh air and the calm of nature," I say, leaning back into him.

"I couldn't agree more. I think this porch would be perfect for a porch swing over there. What do you think?" he asks, his voice full of warmth and joy.

"I've always wanted a porch swing."

"I'll make it happen." He kisses the top of my head.

Later that night, as we are getting ready for bed, I'm in my room, realizing it's been a few nights since I slept in here. I'm gathering pajamas to change into when mine and Jason's wedding photo on my dresser catches my eye.

As I look at the photo of us on our wedding day, I can't help but feel a pang of sadness. We were so young and full of hope back then. Our whole lives ahead of us. But things didn't turn out the way we'd planned.

I never anticipated a life where he wasn't in it. His dying the way he did wasn't even on my radar. It was something that happened to other people, but not us. Now here I am, pregnant with his baby, but living and sleeping with his best friend. What a horrible wife I am.

I can't stare at this photo day in and day out when I'm falling for another man.

And that's just it. I'm falling for Storm, and my feelings for him are already so much stronger than what I felt with Jason, it scares me.

Taking one more look at the wedding photo, I tuck it in the dresser drawer. Because I know it can't last forever, I want to enjoy this time with Storm.

CHAPTER 18

STORM

We have a few days to relax before the trial. I insisted on Jack giving her a break so I could help her destress, with her being pregnant and all.

I have a plan, so I knock on the office door where she has been spending a lot of her time working on Jenna's website. It makes me happy to see her so excited about it.

"Hey, I know your back has been bothering you, so I thought maybe we'd head down to the river. Maybe you can do some swimming to help with your back," I tell her.

"Are you crazy? That water must be freezing!"

"Several hot springs overflow into it, so the river is actually still pretty warm. If nothing else, a good walk will do you good, too."

Even though she looks at me skeptically, she eventually agrees. We get on our swimsuits, grab a couple of towels, and make our way to the river. As we walk, I can see the tension in her body start to fade away. The cool breeze brushes against our faces as we take in the nature around us. I make it a point to name trees and show her some fruit bushes that will bloom in the spring.

The more she knows about the wilderness around her, the safer she and her child will be.

Finally, we reach the river, and I can see her face light up as she takes in the sight before her. The water is crystal clear, and the tinkling sound is pleasant as it rushes over the rocks. Slowly, she undresses, revealing her pregnant belly in her two piece swim suit.

The sight of her makes my heart race and my cock hard.

"You're not getting in?" she asks, looking back at me.

"I'll join you. Right now, I'm just enjoying the view of you getting in." I reply with a grin.

As she slowly steps into the water, she then turns back to look at me with a smile.

"It really is warm!" she giggles.

When she finally lowers herself deeper into the river, I can see the relief on her face.

Joining her in the water, we splash around, laughing and enjoying each other's company. I'm captivated at her beautiful body, the way the water droplets cling to her curves. It's as if all my senses are heightened, and every little detail of her is magnified.

As we playfully splash each other, our bodies brush against one another, and I can feel my hardness pressing against her thighs. She looks up at me with a mix of surprise and lust. There's also desire in her beautiful eyes.

Suddenly, she wraps her arms around my neck and pulls me in for a passionate kiss. Grabbing her ass with my hands, I pull her into me. Just the feeling of her soft lips on mine makes me even more desperate for her.

She breaks the kiss and whispers in my ear, "I need you inside of me right now."

Placing light kisses on her neck, I slowly push my swim trunks down and pull her swimsuit to the side. The water makes it easy to line myself up and slip inside of her. We both moan at how good it feels to be connected again. She wraps her legs around my waist and her arms around my neck and holds on while I thrust in and out of her, driving us both to the edge of pleasure.

"Oh, Storm, that feels so good!" I grab hold of her thighs and thrust even deeper inside of her wet pussy.

She wraps her legs tighter around my waist and pulls me closer to her with each thrust.

As she screams out in pleasure, I can't resist the urge to crash our lips together as we both shudder in ecstasy.

I hold her as she relaxes and comes back to herself. The warm water around us feels so relaxing. As we pull away from each other, I can see the pure happiness in her eyes.

"Thank you for this," she says with a grin.

"Anything for you, baby," I reply, kissing her forehead.

We go back to shore, dry off, and get dressed again before taking the trail back up to the cabin.

"Go finish up the website for the night, and I'll start on dinner," I say when we reach the cabin.

She has been craving red meat the last few days, and I read in the pregnancy book women will crave things based on what their body needs. She might be low on iron, which would explain the red meat cravings, so I have been making sure she gets plenty of it.

Just as dinner is about ready, she joins me in the kitchen.

"Something smells so good." She moves around, setting the table.

"Steak, potatoes, spinach, squash, and the rolls you like," I tell her.

"It sounds delicious. You really do spoil me."

"Well, it is my job to take care of you." I pull her in for a hug.

"Yeah, and you do a really good job."

We sit down and dig into the appetizing food. She gushes all about the website she is making for Jenna, and it's clear she loves what she is doing.

"Do you mind if I go take a bath?" She asks after dinner.

"Of course not. You don't have to ask. You are free to use the tub any time you want."

"I just want to be sure with it being in your room and all."

Setting the plate down that I just brought to the kitchen, I walk over to her. I place my hands on her shoulders and tilt her head up to look at me.

"This is your house too, as much as it is mine. I have nothing to hide, and there is no place on this property off limits to you unless it risks your safety. You don't need permission to go into my room or use the bathtub or to go into the barn or any place else around here," I tell her.

Her eyes are wide, but she nods, "Thank you," she says going off to the bathroom. The entire time I'm cleaning up the kitchen and doing dishes, I'm having to fight imagining her naked in the bathtub. I have to fight thinking about all the things I want to do to her while she's in that bathtub.

Thankfully, she finishes her bath before I finish up with the kitchen. Once I'm done, I go to check on her and find her in her room, folding and putting away clothes that she just pulled from the dryer.

As she moves to put some clothes in the dresser, I instantly notice her picture is missing.

"What happened to your wedding photo?"

She closes the dresser drawer where she had just put some clothes away and turns to look at me.

"With everything we have done and how I feel about you, it didn't seem right to have it out."

My heart races with excitement and a bit of fear about how she feels about me. I take a step toward her.

"And how *do* you feel about me?" She stares into my eyes, and her lips part slightly. I can see the war going on behind her eyes, on what to say and how much to reveal. Moving closer to her, I take her hand and place it on my chest, over my heart, and cover it with mine.

Even though I know she can feel my heart racing, I want her to know how I feel, too. I just don't want to scare her off.

"I think..." she whispers and stops as I wrap my other arm around her waist." I think I'm falling for you."

Right then, I don't think I have ever smiled as big as I do at that minute.

"I hope you are because I'm falling for you too." Then I kiss her with all the passion flowing through me.

She melts into my arms, kissing me back. When we pull away, she looks up at me and places her hand on my cheek.

Picking her up bridal style earns me a squeal as she wraps her hands around my neck. I carry her to my room, gently set her on my bed and lie down beside her.

I lift her shirt just enough to expose her belly to me, and rest my hand on the baby bump.

"Damn, you are even more beautiful like this," I say, kissing my way across her stomach.

She giggles, rubbing my head as I play with her belly button.

It's like her giggles wake up the baby because the next time I place a kiss on the side of her belly, he kicks me pretty hard in the jaw.

"Oh, little man has some strength," I say with a smile.

"I've been looking at names the last few days, trying to see what sounds right."

I move up to lie beside her again. "Have you found any that are standing out to you?" I ask, propping myself on my elbow.

"None that feels right. I've been looking at name lists online, and nothing seems to jump out at me."

"Well, you have time, sweetheart. The right name will come to you at the right time. Don't let it stress you out."

"I know," she says, snuggling up to me, and in no time flat, she is asleep.

I'm left wondering how different things would be if it was my baby she was carrying instead.

CHAPTER 19

RIVER

Tonight is girls' night at Emelie and Axel's cabin. While we girls gather in the living room and kitchen, the guys are in the new family room they added at the back of the cabin. Detective Greer is joining them as well since they might have a few leads on some land for him up here in the mountains.

I'm really excited and nervous to show Jenna the website I made for her photography. I never considered doing anything like this professionally before.

It's been a while since we have all been in the same place like this. The other six girls have known each other longer, but they welcomed me into the group as if I've been around just as long.

"So, Jenna, I have the website up and running if you want to look," I say nervously.

"Oh, absolutely!" She's full of smiles.

Then I set the laptop on the beautiful wood dining room table, Jenna sitting beside me while the other girls gather around us.

"I can't believe you did all of this. River, it's amazing!" Jenna exclaims.

Using the time before dinner, I showed her the ins and outs and how a customer would use the website. Then, I show her on the back end how to update and add new products. I used the picture of the river the other day as my inspiration for it all, and I'm really happy with how it turned out.

"This is amazing, and it's so easy to use!" Emelie says as she flips through it.

"River, I can't thank you enough for all of this. It's as if you just read my mind," Jenna says, her eyes never leaving the screen.

As the guys come in for food, Jenna shows off the website to them. Storm walks up behind me, wrapping his arms around me. Then he proceeds to rub my belly while kissing my neck.

This is the first real PDA he's shown around his friends, and it doesn't go unnoticed by Emelie.

"I'm really impressed by what you did with that website," he whispers in my ear, and I lean into him.

"It was nothing. Nice to help a friend." I say as we get ready for dinner.

We all spread out over the dining room, kitchen, and living room for dinner. The guys serve the girls their food and make sure they have water and whatever else they need. It's nice to see them so protective like this.

Watching Detective Greer, or Evan, as he keeps telling us to call him, I can tell he wants what they all have, too. I got a taste of it with Storm, but this can't last forever. When things are over between us, I know he will be the standard that I measure every guy to from now on.

As we all finish eating, Jenna and her husband Phoenix pull me aside and hand me a white envelope.

"What's this?" I ask, opening it to find a check for over $3,000.

"It's for the website. What you did was more professional than some of the designers I was looking at a few months ago. I did some digging, and this is average for what you can make designing a website like you did. As you make a name for yourself, you can charge much more," Jenna says.

"This is too much!" I gasp.

Not only is this more than Jason made as base pay in the military each month, it only took me a few days to do the website, and it was fun. I can't take her money.

"I knew you would say that, but I looked at the stats, so I won't take no for an answer." Jenna hugs me, and then they walk off as Storm walks up.

"What was that about?" he asks.

"They paid me for doing the website and said it was average what I could make! Storm, it's more than Jason made in a month in the military!" I show him the check.

"Listen, Jenna and Phoenix are not hard up for money. It doesn't look like it, but after his parents died and left him everything, Phoenix is worth billions."

"Still!"

"River, you deserve that money. Jenna and Phoenix recognized that you put a lot of work into that website. Don't feel guilty for being compensated for your time and talent." Taking a deep breath, I lean my head on his chest, and he wraps his arms around me. He's right. I put a lot of effort into it, and it's unfair for me to downplay it.

After everyone is done with dinner, we sit around the fire pit outside. Storm pulls me onto his lap, and we cuddle under a blanket. The warmth from the fire and his body are comforting as we all talk.

Jack sits down beside us and pulls Sage onto his lap as well.

"Hey River, would you be willing to make a website for the shop? I'd love to be able to sell more local stuff online. Since I'm already getting tourists asking to buy stuff when they get home, I could easily send them to my website. That way, I can take on more local items as well. Of course, I'm happy to pay you for your time."

I sit there stunned. I never thought I could make money from something I would do for fun like this. Storm squeezes my hip under the blanket, pulling me from my thoughts.

"I'd love to. Why don't you shoot me an email tomorrow with what you want the website to be able to do, any logos or theme you want to use, and all that?" I say.

"Perfect will do," he says, turning back to the other couples talking around the fire.

"Okay, so it's obvious something is going on between the two of you. It's time to spill the beans," Emelie says to Storm and me.

I feel Storm tense up under me, knowing he is uncomfortable with this sudden attention. But I also know Emelie won't let it go until we tell the truth. I'm not sure what the truth is and what he is willing to reveal.

"We are getting to know each other. I guess you can say dating as of recently. It's all very new, and we will talk about it when we are ready," he says, ending the questioning, and I'm grateful.

"I wanted to ask how you all met and your stories," I say, looking around the fire.

"Axel and Emelie fell first, so they should go first," Sage says.

"I was lost in the woods after my ex-boyfriend left me there on a camping trip. After stumbling on Axel in the river, he let me stay with him as we rode out a storm. By the time the storm was over, I was his." Emelie smiles up at Axel.

"Phoenix and I fell in love next. Right after I moved to town, we met in Jack's store. I had hired him to custom build a dining room table for my cabin, the first real piece of furniture I bought on my own. When I wanted to get some local photos, he showed me around. We fell in love that way," Jenna says.

"Cash and I were next. We actually met in the grocery store where I was using the free Wi-Fi, thanks to Jana. And we just started talking and connected from there. It was right after his brother had died," Hope says. Then Cash, her husband, leans down to kiss her with a big smile on his face.

"Well, I met Cole here because Hope's mom had kidnapped me," Jana says, grinning big.

"What?!" I ask in shock.

"My mom had found out that a cashier had access to money. Because she was a druggie, she was trying to do anything she could to get some of it. Including kidnapping my best friend," Hope says with a sad smile.

"But Cash called on Cole here to help out, and it all worked out for the best. He nursed me back to health after the accident, and we've been inseparable ever since," Jana finishes.

"Bennett and I had a very untraditional start. Due to circumstances after my father's death, I became a mail-order bride, and that's how Bennett found me. But in the time that we were getting to know each other, we fell head over heels in love," Willow says.

I make a note to get more details on their story later.

"We are the most recent love story. I was visiting a friend's cabin, and I didn't know that the cabin had been sold to Jack. He came home, and there I was. Of course, my car wouldn't start, so he was stuck with me for a few days, and by the time we got the part to fix my car, he didn't want me to leave." Sage says, smiling at Jack.

So many great love stories. It really does give me hope.

As the fire crackles, the gratitude I feel for this group of friends washes over me. They've welcomed me with open arms, and I'm finally starting to feel like I belong somewhere. And, of course, there's Storm.

Stealing a glance at him, I catch him looking back at me. His eyes twinkle with mischief, and I couldn't stop the blush that covers my face if I tried.

"Now that the love stories are out of the way, I wanted to see what all of you were doing next weekend," Evan says.

"I guess it depends upon what you need," Jack says.

"Well, my best friend and his brothers have opened a whiskey distillery in town and are having their big grand opening. And I was hoping you all would go with me and show some support. They've had a rough time opening the distillery, and I think they could use it."

"That sounds like fun. We will be there," Jack says.

I look at Storm, and he nods, and I turn back to Evan. "We will be there as well."

Everyone agrees, and we decide to meet at Jack's shop. That way we can all go together since the distillery is downtown and a few blocks from Jacks's store just off Main Street.

As the fire dies down, Storm and I say good-night to everyone and go back to our cabin.

Once inside, we kick off our shoes. Storm starts a fire in the fireplace, and I curl up in front of the fire, the warmth of the flames surrounding us.

"I really enjoy spending time with everyone like that, and I hope to do it more," I tell him.

"We can make it a regular thing. But try to keep them away once the baby is born? Not happening. They won't give you a moment's peace," he says, smiling.

That sounds nice to me, considering how few friends I've had until now.

takes the envelope and smiles as Jack goes back to the front of the store.

When she opens the envelope, she gasps.

"Storm! This is more than double what Jenna paid me!" she says in shock.

That's when Jack peeks his head back in.

"And that website is more complicated than Jenna's, and I'm willing to bet it took you longer to do, didn't it?" he says,

River just nods her head.

"Charge what you are worth. Also, here is the card for the bakery next door. They are wanting you to redo their website as well. If you are up for it, I have a few other connections that could use someone who is more budget friendly," Jack says, handing her a business card to the bakery.

"I'd be happy to help them out," River says in awe.

"Make sure to create yourself a website to show off what you can do so we can help promote you. Keep it up, and you will be drowning in more work than you can keep up with," Jack says before returning to the front if the store.

When Jack leaves us, River just stares at the check. Then she sits somewhat dazedly on the couch next to me.

"I... I was hoping to find a way to stay home with the baby. Not only did I not want to send him to daycare, but have you seen the prices? Now I can possibly think about giving up on that idea..." "If you want to stay home with him, then we will make it happen. You have plenty of built in babysitters here too. I promise there is no reason for daycare." "If this takes off, I can work at home and not worry about daycare."

Since all I know about website design is self-taught, it never crossed my mind that I could get paid so well for it."

"That doesn't matter. What matters is what you can do. Show it off and people won't care if you went to school for it or not."

As some of the couples join us, they pull her in for a hug. They all gush over the site River made for Jack while we wait for everyone to get here.

Finally, we are together and make our way to the distillery grand opening with Evan. The excitement in the air is palpable.

The wind whips through River's hair, and the excitement on her face is obvious. It's as if I can see the gears turning in her head. I know she's already thinking about taking on new clients. Hell, with the amount Jack just paid her, I don't blame her for wanting to pursue her passion further.

The grand opening is in full swing by the time we arrive. It's packed with people, all chatting and laughing over the sounds of a live band.

"Hey guys, this is my buddy, Cody. He and his three brothers run this place," Evan introduces us.

Cody is a tall and rugged man who looks like he could handle himself in the mountains. He has a beaming smile as he shakes our hands and welcomes us to the grand opening. The way he talks, I can tell that he is proud of what his family has built, and the love and care they have put into every aspect of their operation.

Eagerly, Cody takes us on a tour of the distillery. As we walk through the maze of copper stills and aging barrels, River's eyes light up with excitement. She is asking questions and is really interested in how they do what they do.

Finishing the tour, Cody leads us to a tasting room filled with the rich aroma of whiskey. We take a seat at the bar, and he pours each of us a sample of the distillery's flagship brand.

"Take a sip," River says. "Let me know what you think. We will have to come back after the baby is born so I can try it."

I'm already planning a date here once the baby is a bit older.

The whiskey is smooth on my tongue with notes of smoky oak, caramel, and dark fruit, followed by a gentle smokiness that lingers for a moment on my tongue. All in all, this is one of the best whiskeys I've ever had.

"It's good. Smoky with a hint of caramel in it. But damn, that it one of the best I've ever tasted," I say, making both Cody and River smile.

"That's what we like to hear. It's a family recipe that has been passed down for generations. It started in the hills of Tennessee and was brought to Montana a few generations ago," Cody says.

As we make our way around the distillery, admiring the different blends and aging processes, River seems to relax into the atmosphere. The excitement of the grand opening had dissipated any nervousness she had felt earlier about her newfound success.

"This is incredible," she says, running her hand along the copper still. "I never knew making alcohol could be so... romantic."

I chuckle. "Romantic, huh?"

"I mean it," River says, looking at me with a glint in her eye. "The way they've poured their hearts into this place and the passion they have for their craft, it's inspiring."

As we finish up the tour, Cody invites us to try one final blend, a limited-edition whiskey that they only release once a year.

"This one's got a bit of a kick to it," Cody says with a grin. "We call it the 'Mountainside Fire.'"

When I take a sip, I can feel the heat spreading through my chest. It's strong, but there's a sweetness to it that balances it out perfectly.

Cody shares the story of how his grandfather had come up with the recipe, and there's pride in his voice as he talks about the family tradition.

Emelie takes a sip, and her eyes widen in surprise. "Oh my god, this is amazing."

"I told you," Cody says with a grin, taking a sip of his own. "It's one of our best. Only a few hundred bottles made it out this year."

As we finish trying out the final blend, I feel River's hand slip into mine. She looks at me with a smile, her eyes sparkling with desire.

"I'm ready to head home," she whispers.

We make our way out of the distillery and walk towards the car. The late afternoon sun stretched out above us. As we drive back towards the cabin, I feel River's hand on my thigh, her touch sending shivers down my spine.

I pull into the cabin's driveway and quickly turn off the engine. River wastes no time in climbing over the center console and straddling my lap, her lips crashing onto mine. Even though she barely fits with her belly, actually she really fits perfectly. I deepen the kiss, my hands gripping her waist firmly, and she moans into my mouth.

"I want you," she whispers, breaking away from the kiss and looking at me with a lustful gaze.

Without hesitation, I lift her up and carry her towards the bedroom. She giggles as she wraps her arms around my neck, her legs clenched around my waist.

Once inside the room, I gently place her on the bed, my lips never leaving hers for a second. We spend the next few hours exploring each other's bodies, and I can tell from the way she moves that this is one experience she won't be forgetting any time soon.

When the sun is just beginning to set, we finally settle down into each other's arms. It's the most bittersweet experience in the world. I know that our time together is fleeting, but I'm still so grateful for what time we have.

Chapter 21

River

Today is the first court date. Jack has warned me there could be several of them, depending on how long the other side tries to draw this out. I'm just hoping Jason's parents aren't actually in the courtroom. The thought of them being this close to me scares me.

Montana has felt like my safe bubble because I'm so far from them. It's been my safe haven during all this, and now the bubble is bursting. When we get to the courthouse, Jack is already there, and so are the other couples. Storm's mom and stepdad said they would slip in the back unnoticed once we begin so as not to draw attention.

Entering the crowded courthouse, I can feel my anxiety start to build. Storm has a re-assuring hand on my back, and I cling to his other for stability. We make our way to the front of the room and take our seats. Storm sits right behind me, close enough I can reach out and take his hand anytime I need it.

Soon, Jason's parents enter and take their seats on the other side of the aisle. My heart rate spikes and I feel like I'm going to be sick. These are the people who are trying to take my baby. My baby who hasn't even been born yet. Protectively, I wrap my hand around my belly. I will do anything to keep them from being in my son's life. Even if it means fleeing the country.

That's a thought I haven't voiced out loud yet. But if I leave and the baby is born else-where, he won't be an American citizen. I'm going to need to do some research discrete-ly. Just to have the knowledge in my back pocket.

I try not to look to the other side of the court for Jason's parents. That way I can pretend they aren't here.

The judge enters the room, and everyone rises. My eyes follow him to his seat as he calls the court into session. As I listen to the legal jargon exchanged by the lawyers, my heart is racing. It's like a foreign language to me, and my anxiety is growing every second. I don't even know what they're fighting about anymore. I just know that I want to win.

I do my best to focus on what Jack and the other lawyer are saying. But every now and then, my gaze involuntarily drifts towards Jason's parents. They look so put-together, so ordinary. Nothing like the monsters I've conjured up in my mind. It's easy to forget by how normal they look that they're the same people who are trying to take my baby away from me.

There seems to be a lot of talk of entering evidence. There is no jury, so this isn't happening like the court shows I've seen on TV. Once the lawyers seem to be done talking to the judge, I get called to the stand to answer questions.

Taking a deep breath, I approach the stand. My hands are shaking, and my heart is pounding so hard that I can feel it in my ears. I remind myself to speak confidently and clearly, to not let them see how scared I am.

"River, can you tell us about your relationship with Jason?" Jack asks, his eyes gentle.

I take a deep breath and begin to speak. "Jason and I met in school. We were friends first for a few years and then started dating our junior year. When he joined the military, he asked me to marry him. I said yes, and we were married after boot camp. He was assigned his first duty station in Virginia Beach."

"And to the best of your understanding, what kind of relationship did Jason have with his parents?" Jack asks.

"Objection, speculation." the other lawyer says.

"Overruled," the judge says, turning back to me.

"When we were in school before he joined the military, he had an okay relationship with his parents. Even though they weren't around much, they did have family dinners a few nights a month. They kept pushing him to do stuff he didn't want to after school. Once he joined the military, they disowned him and then once we were married, they cut off all communication. They weren't at his boot camp graduation or any of his deployments or homecomings. They didn't even attend his funeral."

"Did Jason try to reach out to them?" Jack asks.

"Many times, phone calls went unanswered. When we were cleaning out his office, we found stacks of letters that were returned to sender."

"Those were submitted to evidence," Jack tells the judge who makes some notes on the paper in front of her.

Then Jack asks some more questions before turning the questioning over to the other lawyer. The lawyer's voice is condescending as he asks me about my relationship with Jason, making it sound like I'm nothing more than a one-night stand. I feel myself getting angry but push the feeling down. Reminding myself that I need to stay calm.

The questioning continues for what feels like hours. My stomach is churning, and I can barely keep my composure. Then he asks the question I've been waiting for.

"And how do you plan to support the child without a job?" he asks.

I smile, knowing I have an answer.

For the first time I look at Storm's parents, who are also both smiling. George winks at me before I look back at the other lawyer.

"Well, I recently got a job, so employment is not even an issue," I say.

For a moment, he looks stunned like I just messed up his ace in the hole.

"Doing what, Mrs. Owens?" he recovers.

"Building websites." I give a little info, waiting for him to dig a hole just like Jack and George taught me.

"Starting up some little company isn't providing enough to support you and a child. It takes time to build up a clientele. What about health insurance for both the child and you?"

"I already have two jobs each paying me more than Jason got in a month from the military. Thanks to word of mouth, I have three more lined up. My website and portfolio just launched yesterday, and as of this morning I already have a few email inquiries. Regarding insurance, I'm sure you know surviving spouses and children get VA medical insurance for life. So that won't ever be a concern for us. The VA covers one-hundred percent of our medical care."

That throws him for a loop, and he fumbles through the stack of documents in front of him. A bead of sweat appeared on his forehead and he concedes defeat, asking for a recess. The judge bangs her gavel and declares court adjourned for the day. We commence again on Monday, four days from now.

Pure relief fills me as everyone stands. Storm's parents will slip out the door and meet us at Jack's shop. Previously. We all have planned to meet there and talk about how court went.

I walk over to Jack and Storm on shaky legs.

"Great job, River," Jack says, patting my back. "You held your own up there."

Storm takes my hand and squeezes it tight. "I knew you could do it," he says with a smile.

I feel tears forming in my eyes, and I blink them away. "Thanks to both of you," I say. "I couldn't have done it without your help."

"We're not done yet," Jack interjects. "We still have Monday to get through."

I nod, knowing that the next day in court will be just as nerve-wracking as today was.

On the drive to Jack's shop, Storm is quiet. He is holding my hand, but he seems to understand I need some time to decompress, too. When we get to the shop, Storm parks the car and comes around to open my door, immediately pulling me into his arms.

I breathe in the fresh mountain air, hoping the crispness will clear my mind. This case has been taking its toll on me, and I need to find my center again. I melt into Storm's embrace, feeling his strong arms surround me like a warm blanket.

Burying my face into his chest, I take deep breaths to calm down. He rubs circles on my back, his touch soothing. "You did amazing, River," he murmurs into my hair. "I'm so proud of you."

"Thank you," I whisper, feeling a weight lift off my shoulders. "I'm so glad you guys were there with me."

"Always," he says firmly, giving me a squeeze. "Let's go inside and talk about what's next."

I nod, taking strength from his words. Storm's parents greet us with hugs as we enter the shop. They're so kind and supportive, and once again I feel a surge of gratefulness that Storm has such a wonderful family.

George pulls me aside and hands me a glass of water. "You did a great job in there," he says, clinking his glass against mine in a toast. "I have no doubt that we'll win this case come Monday."

Taking a sip of the water, I feel warmth spread through my body at his words. "Thank you, George. I really appreciate all your help."

"Of course, my dear," he says with a smile. "Now, let's talk about a strategy for Monday. We need to be prepared for anything."

We spend the next hour going over every possible scenario that could happen in court, from the opposition's arguments to the judge's potential questions. Jack and George make sure that I'm fully prepared for anything that might come my way, and

I feel more confident by the time we're finished.

Yet I feel more vulnerable and exposed than I ever have in my life. The fate of my life, and my child, is in the hands of a judge who knew nothing about me until today. How the hell is any of this fair?

CHAPTER 22

STORM

River was exhausted after court yesterday, so I let her sleep in because she obviously needs it. But now that it's after eleven in the morning, I'm a little worried, so I go to our bedroom to check on her.

The sight that greets me takes my breath away. She's still asleep, but her leg is on full display from under the sheets, and her creamy skin is begging to be touched.

She is on her side, hugging a pillow that's supporting her belly. Her thick hair is fanned out behind her, and the slight blush on her cheeks gives her a healthy glow.

Grabbing my phone, I take a picture of her in our bed like this. I want to remember this moment. Safe and blissful. I walk over to the side of the bed, kneeling down so my face is next to her, and gently start rubbing her arm.

"River, Sweetheart. It's time to get up," I say.

At my words, she begins to stir. When she opens her eyes, they lock on me.

I'm frozen. She is stunning, even sleepy like this. I know I want this every day.

"What time is it?" she asks, rolling onto her back.

"After eleven," I tell her, pushing some hair from her face.

"I don't know why I'm so tired. I never sleep this long." She stretches her body languidly.

The thin fabric of her shirt tightens over her breasts, revealing her hard nipples under it.

"Take your time and get up. I'll make you something to eat," I say. All the while ignoring how hard she is making me. She obviously needs rest, and I plan to allow her to get plenty as soon as I feed her and the baby.

I'm making pancakes when she comes out of the bedroom.

"Storm?" She sounds panicked, so I drop what I'm doing and turn to look at her.

"I'm bleeding," she cries.

"Okay, where did you cut yourself? I have a first aid kit under the sink," I say, walking to her and looking for a cut or scrape.

"No, I didn't cut myself. I'm bleeding like my period," she cries.

"Let's get you dressed and down to the doctor. You go get clothes on, and I'll make the call.

I call the doctor who will be waiting for us to get to her clinic since it's closer than the nearest hospital. Also, I decide to call my buddy Cole. He was a medic in the military and the reason I moved out here to Whiskey River. He'll know what to do, and his wife, Jana, will alert the others as to what is going on.

Once she is dressed, I help her to the car, and neither of us says a word the entire ride into town. Holding her hand tightly, I want to let her know I'm here for her just as much as I need to know she is okay.

As we pull up to the clinic, I can see the worry etched on River's face. Even though I wish with all my heart I could take away her fear and pain, all I can do is be here for her. We walk through the doors and are immediately greeted by the receptionist. After explaining our situation, we're taken back to a room.

My thoughts are racing. I caused this. I know it in my gut. We shouldn't have been having sex. I was having sex with my best friend's *wife*. What the hell is wrong with me? I could have injured her or the baby.

As we wait for the doctor to arrive, River and I sit in silence, both lost in our own thoughts. She's holding onto my hand so tightly that I can feel her nails digging into my skin. I try to reassure her that every-thing will be all right, but my own doubts are making it hard to speak with conviction.

I don't leave her side as she changes into the gown and gets ready for the doctor, who thankfully doesn't make us wait.

"Okay, let's see what is going on," she says and first pulls out the Doppler and easily finds the baby's heartbeat.

"His heartbeat is good and strong. That's a good sign. Let me check you out and see if anything pops out, okay?"

All we can do is nod. Words escape us.

"Nothing out of the ordinary. I'd like a nurse to come in and draw some blood to run some tests. How much blood was it that you saw?" the doctor asks.

"It wasn't much. Like my period was trying to start?" River says.

"All right, what have you been doing the last three days or so? Any heavy lifting? Lots of walking?" the doctor asks.

"No more walking than normal. I did have the first court date yesterday. The baby's grandparents are trying to sue for custody."

"That will do it. The stress of something like that can easily cause you to bleed. I understand that you can't avoid this, but minimizing the stress involved is tough. I recommend bed rest and zero other stressors in your life at home." The doctor looks at me, making it clear that I am to make sure she has nothing else to stress about.

"I can do that. But what about court? She has to be there again on Monday," I say.

"Keep her on complete bed rest other than to get up and use the restroom. Until Monday, I don't even want her to moving around. When you need to get ready for court, take a shower and do what you have to do to prepare. Once you're in the courtroom, try to stay seated as much as possible and come home immediately. Then, back on bed rest until I can see you again in a week. We will re-evaluate you then." The doctor says all this firmly, leaving no room for negotiations.

As we leave the clinic and get back into the car, silence hangs heavily between us. I don't know what to say or how I can help, but I know that I need to be there for her.

I made Jason a promise, and I've done nothing but violate his trust these last several weeks. I wasn't able to protect Jason on his last deployment, and I have to live with the fact.

But now, I have to protect River and the baby growing inside of her. I can't let anything happen to them. When we pull into the driveway, I help her out of the car and into the house.

Once we get inside, Cole and Jana are waiting for us.

"Are you okay? What did the doctor say?" Jana says, rushing to me and helping me get River to the couch.

"She said it was stress from everything going on and that I need to be on the best rest until she sees me again next week," River says, setting her feet on the coffee table.

"What about court on Monday?" Cole asks.

"She said I can go but should remain seated and as relaxed as possible."

"Well, let's get you to bed. We can talk there," Jana says.

I'm up and making sure she gets comfortable in bed. Then I leave her to talk to Jana as Cole, and I go outside to work with the dogs.

In order to still keep my promise to my best friend, I can't pursue any kind of relationship with her. This was the Universe telling me that in the worst way possible. The hardest thing is that I still have to tell her and let her down as gently as possible. She has to know we can't keep going like this. Jason never would have asked me to take care of her if he thought for even a second this would happen.

"I can see your mind working. Don't make any big choices right now. She has too much going on," Cole says.

"I know. I just worry I piled on to the stress, and that's the last thing I ever wanted to do."

Cole stares at me for a moment. "That's not all of it. You know I'm not one to open up, so I won't force you to, but just know I'm here to talk if you want."

"Thanks, man. I'll take you up on that once I get my thoughts sorted out."

He stays, helping until Jana comes out, saying River fell asleep. They head home, and after I finish their training, I go inside and start on dinner. The whole time, I was thinking about what I was going to say to her. I know we have to have this talk, and it should be tonight. I don't want to lead her on.

So once dinner is done, I plate it up, put it on a tray, and go to my room where she has been resting.

"It smells amazing. I didn't realize how hungry I was until just now." She sits up and puts her back against the headboard.

"How are you feeling?" I ask, sitting at the foot of the bed to keep plenty of space between us. If she notices, she doesn't say anything.

"I'm doing well. When I was in the bathroom, it looked like the bleeding had stopped. I've just been watching some TV and reading. Trying not to be bored lying in bed," she says, taking her first bite of the pasta dish that I made.

"Listen, I want to talk to you about something that's been on my mind since we went to the doctor," I say. Though I'm not able to meet her gaze as I continue. "I really like you, but I think while all this is going on, we should put things on pause. I would never do anything to harm you or the baby, and I think everything is just piling on you right now, and that's the last thing I want."

She doesn't answer me right away, and when I look up at her, she has a soft, thoughtful look on her face.

"I understand," she says gently, letting me think she understands what I'm not saying.

CHAPTER 23

RIVER

I'm back in court today for round two, and Jason's mom is taking the stand. I'm trying not to let the stress get to me. The last thing I want is to cause any harm to my baby, especially after the last session in court. Storm swears it was more stressful because I was the one on trial and that this time, I should be able just to relax and watch.

At least when I was on the stand, in a way I was in control of the situation. But being just a spectator meant someone else was in control, and that stressed me out just as much, if not more.

As I sit in the courtroom, I can't help but feel the weight of the entire situation bearing down on me. The judge enters the courtroom, and Jack makes an update to the court.

"As you can see, my client has been given a special chair in order to keep her legs up. The stress from this trial has caused her to start bleeding, and her doctor has ordered her on bed rest. She also gave further instructions to keep my client's feet up while here. Due to this, we will be adding to our countersuit emotional distress for her and her unborn child. We reserve the right should this cause any complications to the pregnancy to further our claim. The doctors' paperwork and photographic evidence have been submitted to the court this morning." Jack comes out swinging.

The judge nods, looking at me with a hint of sympathy. I can feel the other side's legal team glaring at me, but I refuse to back down. I know I did nothing wrong, and I'll fight tooth and nail to prove that.

"Just breathe," Storm whispers from behind me.

I nod, thankful for his presence. It's only a matter of time before the proceedings begin, and I try to focus on something else to keep my nerves at bay.

Against my better judgment, I glance over at Jason's mom, who looks smug. I try not to let it get to me, but it's hard. She's been against me from the start, and I can't seem to shake the feeling that she'll do anything to take my baby away from me.

I watch as Jason's mom walks up to the stand. She looks so composed and confident, an air of arrogance radiating off of her. While I try to tell myself that I am in control and that I can handle this, my anxiety only seems to increase the longer I stay here.

Her lawyer asks her some pretty basic questions. Things like if she thinks I'll make a good mother. Of course, she says no. He asks if she thinks I lied about not having a substance abuse problem. Of course, she said yes, and Jack interjected that a simple drug test would put that rumor to rest. She was asked if I had lied about Storm not having PTSD. Once again, she said that I lied about that, too.

When she made the last few comments, Jack rose and said that my medical paperwork had been submitted, and he agreed to submit to any testing that the court orders.

When it's Jack's turn to question her, I find myself getting excited. Jack is good at what he does but seemed overly enthusiastic about this question today.

"Mrs. Owens, is it true that your house is currently in the foreclosure process?" Jack asks.

"I... Well... yes," she stutters.

"Foreclosure information is public, so it doesn't take a genius to follow the money. You thought taking Jason's baby meant you would get the money that the military pays out." Jack pauses to let the emotions play out on Jason's mom's face.

"What you didn't realize is that money is from a life insurance policy, and Jason can assign it to whoever he wants. It doesn't automatically go to the child. So, as Jason was getting ready for deployment, he specifically signed that money over to his wife, the same with the additional life insurance policy he took out. It was specifically signed over to his wife. So even if you were to gain custody of the child, you would have no legal right to either of those payments as they were not given to his child." Jack hands some papers to the man who has been running evidence between the lawyers and the judge.

My eyes stay glued on Jason's mom, whose face goes pale.

"Is it also true that your husband has racked up significant gambling debt yet again? A problem he's been treated for and swore that he'd stop. Then paid off all prior debts just to have piled on more gambling debts," Jack says.

"He hasn't been gambling again. That is a past issue that he has sought help for," she counters.

"In my hand is a stack of bills of places that he owes money from people that he's borrowed from. These are just the legitimate places. How is this any different than you trying to claim that River is an unfit mother because her parents do drugs? Even though she's never once touched them and hasn't been around her parents since she was a young child?" Jack again hands papers to the man to take up to the judge.

"We'd like to request a recess to review the new evidence," the other lawyer says.

"I will grant it because I need to review all this paperwork myself. The court will convene on Wednesday. Any objections?" the judge asks.

"Is it possible to do Thursday, as River has a follow-up with her doctor on Wednesday? Once you review the paperwork, you will see the date has been set," Jack asks.

"That's fine, Thursday it is. Let's try to wrap this up then," the judge says. Then she smacks down her gavel, and a loud echo fills the quiet courtroom.

Once the judge exits the room, there's a flurry of activity of people talking, paper shuffling, and people moving.

Like last time, I know Storm's parents were in the back and one of the first people out. But this time, we're all meeting back at Storm's place to go over everything so that I can continue to obey the bed rest orders. The girls insist on cooking and stocking the freezer for us for the next week or so. And I'm pretty sure the guys will take any excuse just to get together and shoot the shit.

When the courtroom has cleared out, Storm walks over and helps me out to his truck. Unlike last time, he didn't hold my hand on the way back to the cabin. I can feel the distance between us, and I know he's got some guilt over everything that's happening.

As soon as he started to voice his concerns, I felt the guilt crash into me as well. I think that's something we both have to deal with, which is why I'm not putting up too big of a fight.

Being on bed rest has given me a lot of time to think, maybe more time than I should be allowed. But I've come to realize that I need to be out on my own for no reason other than to prove to myself that I can.

One decision that is firm is I want to stay here in Whiskey River. I didn't want to be far from Storm and the friends that I am making. My whole support system is here. As soon as the doctor gives me an okay to be up and moving around, I want to head into town and start looking at places.

Even though I know my choices will be limited, I'm sure I can find something. Since I already have a small waiting list of clients wanting me to do their websites, I'm not concerned with having enough income to get a small two-bedroom apartment above one of the buildings downtown. Being downtown will allow me to walk almost anywhere I need, and then I only have to use a vehicle to come up the mountain to visit Storm and my friends.

As soon as we get home, Shadow is right there, sniffing me and wanting to make sure I'm okay. He's been lying in bed with me and snuggling with me since Storm spent that first night on the couch. It was then I moved back to my room. It's crazy how quickly I got used to not sleeping alone again. Thankfully, with Shadow, I'm not.

"Okay, let's get you to the couch," Storm says as we pull up to the cabin.

As we get inside, Storm's mom has already set up the couch with some pillows and blankets for me, and I settle right in.

"Do you really think we can wrap this up on Thursday?" I ask Jack once everyone has arrived.

"I believe so if the judge is adamant about it. The other side could try to keep post-poning or adding to the case, but I think, at this point, it just hurts them. The judge knows all this is causing harm to the baby, and I don't think she will let it go on much longer. My guess is she will have a decision in mind when we walk on Thursday. Unless they have some big jaw dropper to add, she will just want to wrap things up," Jack says.

"I agree. This judge is known for not letting trials drag on. And she's a mother, so she will have more empathy toward wanting to make sure the baby is healthy and being with the right person. So I think she'll wrap this up as quickly as possible," George adds.

The guys move to talking strategy in the kitchen, and the girls pile into the living room with me.

"Did you see her face when she realized she wouldn't be getting any of the money?" Hope says, shaking her head.

"Always follow the money. We learned that the hard way, didn't we?" Jana says, squeezing Hope's hand.

"I'm just glad he found information he could use in court. I know not all Jack's research is on the up and up."

"Oh shit!" Storm's voice fills the cabin, and everyone goes quiet.

"Well, don't keep up on our toes!" Willow says to them, and Storm, Jack, and George walk over to us.

"I've been having my assistant do some digging on Jason's parents, and she just sent me an email with a gold mine," George says, still scrolling on his phone.

"Well?" Storm's mom says, her impatience audible.

"A lawsuit was just filed a few days ago against Jason's dad for sexual harassment. This isn't the first. He's settled a few others out of court to keep them hush hush. I'd say that's a very unsuitable environment for a child, don't you?" George smirks.

I rest my head back on one of the pillows, the day catching up with me. I must drift off because the next thing I know, I open my eyes to see Storm's mom holding a tray of pastries and a glass of water. A smile lights up her face as she sees me awake.

"Hello, dear. Have a good rest?" she asks as she sets the tray on my lap.

"I'm doing okay, thank you," I reply, taking a sip of the water.

Everyone seems to have left but his mom and stepdad.

"I'm sorry I feel asleep," I say, taking one of the cookies from the tray.

"It's okay. They all understand you need your sleep. Storm just needed some help in the barn, so George stayed back to help because he also didn't want to leave you alone if you happened to wake up," she says, smiling.

Typical Storm. Even when we are putting distance between us, he is still taking care of me.

CHAPTER 24

RIVER

Waiting in the exam room for the doctor to tell me everything I've been doing has helped my baby is the longest wait of my life. Typically, Storm is right beside me, holding my hand. Today, he's sitting on the other side of the room, pretty much as far away from me as he can get.

Even though I try to catch his eye, Storm avoids looking at me. He's been acting more and more distant the past few days, and I'm not entirely sure why. I can guess why, but I hate thinking I'm right. It's been bothering me and making me feel uneasy.

I take a deep breath and try to focus on the present moment.

There is a knock on the door, and in comes the doctor.

"Alright, let's listen to your baby and do a quick exam. Your blood work from last time is good, and your hormones are strong. I'd like to take another blood sample and compare the two, then send you for an ultrasound as well. We will go from there," she says, smiling.

Nodding my head, I'm silently thanking the heavens that everything seems to be okay so far. The doctor carefully places the cold gel on my swollen belly and begins to move the wand around. I can hear the whooshing sound of my baby's heartbeat, and tears gather in my eyes. Storm reaches over and takes my hand, squeezing it tightly.

"It sounds good," the doctor says, smiling. "He has a nice strong heartbeat, and everything looks great. Let's get you to Ultrasound, and then we will meet back here and chat, okay?" she says, wiping gel from my belly.

We follow a nurse down to the ultrasound room. It is dimly lit and has a relaxing vibe. I lay on the exam table while the nurse applies more cold gel to my belly. Storm sits quietly in the chair beside me, fidgeting with his hands.

The image screen flickers to life, revealing the black and white image of my baby. Tears prick my eyes as I stare at the tiny human growing inside of me.

"Let's take some measurements," she says, moving the wand around to get a better view.

Storm stands beside me, and I can feel the tension radiating off of him. When I squeeze his hand in an attempt to comfort him, he doesn't seem to respond. My heart aches to see him like this, but I know I can't force him to talk to me if he doesn't want to.

The nurse finishes the ultrasound, and we make our way back to the exam room to wait for the doctor. I catch Storm's eye this time, but he quickly looks away. My mind races with worries and doubts.

When the doctor walks in, she is all smiles.

"Your baby looks healthy and happy. He's growing and right on track. I say you can get off bed rest but no long walks, hiking, carrying every item, or strenuous exercises. If you feel tired, nap. If your feet start to swell, you need to put them up. Take it easy, and I want to see you again next week, okay?"

Relief floods over me at the good news.

No sooner are we in the truck when Storm's phone rings.

"Hey, Jack." He answers, all friendly, but after a moment, his whole demeanor changes before he turns to me.

"Do you know a Brett Gibbons?" Storm asks.

"Yeah, Jason served with him. They were friends. Why?" I ask.

"He's at Jack's shop asking for you." Storm answers, his voice tight and controlled.

Jack's shop is still my forwarding address, so it makes sense he'd show up there if he was trying to find me. The question is, why is he looking for me?

"Let's go see what he wants. He didn't come all this way for nothing," I say.

Storm doesn't look too happy, but he nods.

"Tell him to hang tight. We will be there in less than twenty minutes," Storm says.

"It doesn't take twenty minutes to get there," I say when Storm hangs up.

"No, but you haven't eaten, so I'm stopping at the cafe to grab you a sandwich," he says as my stomach rumbles, proving his point.

As we pull up to Jack's shop, my heart races with nerves and curiosity. What could Brett Gibbons possibly want from me? When I step out of the truck, Storm takes my hand, leading me towards the shop.

Walking inside, I immediately recognize the man standing by the counter. Brett Gibbons looks just as I remember him: tall and muscular with short, blonde hair and piercing blue eyes that seem to light up when he sees me.

"River. You look good!" When he steps up to hug me, I can feel the tension rolling off Storm.

"I am so sorry about Jason. I was injured in the same incident and was laid up in the hospital, or else I'd have been at the funeral," he says, suddenly sober.

"I know you would have. So would the rest of the unit." I squeeze his hand for reassurance. Yes, I lost my husband, but he also lost a friend and a brother-in-arms.

"Listen, I'm sorry I couldn't get out here before. Like I said, I was injured, and I wasn't cleared to fly, and this felt like something I should do in person. Jason knew we were going into a dangerous situation. We all did. So, we wrote letters home and gave them to each other in the event..." he clears his throat. His meaning is clear in case the worst happens.

"Jason wrote this for you." He pulls an envelope out of his pocket.

My heart beats quickly when Brett hands me the envelope. My hand shakes as I take it from him, but I don't have the strength to read it right now.

We catch up for a while, before he needs to head out to get back and catch his plane home. His wife is also pregnant, but wasn't able to travel with him. It goes without saying that he doesn't want to be away from her any longer than he needs to be. He sounds just like Jason.

"Do you want to read that here, or do you want to go home?" Jason asks once Brett leaves, and the shop is quiet.

"Home," I whisper as my mind starts racing.

I am holding the last thing Jason touched. His last thoughts and words to me and I can't bring myself to open it.

Storm leads me out of the shop and helps me into the truck. The silence is palpable as we drive home, each lost in our own thoughts. When we arrive at the cabin, I go straight to my bedroom. Closing the door behind me, I sit on the bed with Shadow beside me, clutching the envelope with trembling hands.

Shadow seems to know what is going on and keeps his head in my lap, offering me comfort as I try to find the strength to open the letter. I'm equal parts excited to see what Jason has to say and at the same time, terrified of what I will read.

Finally, I take a deep breath and begin to open the letter slowly, savoring the weight of it in my trembling hands. I can feel the tears threatening to spill from my eyes as I read his familiar handwriting. Reading his words, the memories come flooding back to me. Memories of our life together and all the love we shared.

River,

If you are reading this, I am so, so sorry, my love.

I knew going on this was a dangerous mission, and I did everything I could to fight my way back to you, but it looks like fate has other plans for us.

Take comfort in knowing that I died doing what I loved, serving my country. But my true love will always be you, River.

Just like I promised, I did everything I could to set you up to be taken care of. From the life insurance from the military, to the extra life insurance policy I took out. They are all yours. Use them for your future and our child's future.

I keep thinking of everything I want to say to you. Things like how much I love you, how happy you make me, and how I don't regret a single second of our lives together.

Then I think of how you have to move on without me, and I want you to be happy. Just know Storm is going to be there for you and our child. He isn't doing it out of duty. He truly cares about you, and he will protect you and our child at all costs. Don't pass that up. You will need a support system.

I want you to fall in love, the kind of love that makes you cry at the end of the movie. What we had was a different kind of love. You are my soul mate, but I'm not sure I'm your only soul mate.

There was always this spark between you and Storm that neither of you seemed to notice. Don't dismiss it. I needed the military to get away from my parents, to support you, and find where I belong. I know that I was meant to protect and provide for you as long as I was alive, and this is how I was able to do it.

Storm never needed the military like I did. He is strong, and he knows who he is. He's stable and steadfast. In Montana, he's set up a good life, and if he's the one you fall in love with, I couldn't think of a better man to raise my child.

Don't mourn me too long. I want you to smile and be happy again when the baby is born. I don't want there to be a dark cloud over that moment. But know I will be there with you, cheering you on and supporting you the whole way.

Let our child know I loved them with my whole heart and will be watching over them every day, and I will be there at every event in their lives.

Going forward, I want you to know you were the one thing I chose for myself. My parents planned every little aspect of my life, but you were mine. Over and over again, I'd make the same choice. I don't regret one moment of our time together, and looking back, I should have let you paint our bedroom pink.

Inside this envelope is a letter to Storm and also one for my parents should you need it.

I love you with all my heart and soul.

Your husband,

Jason

When I'm done with the letter, I let go and wail. I cry out my pain, my loss, and our baby's loss. The pain is so bad my heart hurts. This is what I expected to feel at the funeral and the days following.

But I didn't anticipate feeling it now, in my own bedroom, with only Shadow to bear witness to my grief. I clutch the letter to my chest and let the sobs wrack my body. I can feel Shadow trying to comfort me, licking away my tears and pressing his body close to mine.

I don't hear my door open or Storm entering. Even as I cry, Storm is lying behind me on the bed and holding me tight. He doesn't speak, he just holds me. Even when he's trying to pull away from me, he's there when I need him, and I know he always will be.

That's when I know I can't stay here, not even until the baby is born.

CHAPTER 25

STORM

River spent most of the night crying, and I have never felt so helpless in all my life. All I could do was hold her. I have no idea what was in the letter she got, no idea what Jason's final words to her were, but what I do have is the letter he wrote to me.

One that let me know that River was his soul mate, though he didn't think he was hers. He says he thinks I was. We always got along better, and he wants me to know if things work between River and me, I have his whole-hearted support. He said he couldn't imagine anyone better to raise his kid.

I pride myself on being able to stay composed in challenging situations. But when I say I lost it, I don't think I've ever broken down the way I had after reading that letter.

Having his support is what I needed to break down that final wall between River and me. Only now, her walls are up. She has every intention of heading into town next week to go look at apartments. It's her intention to be out of the cabin before the baby is born.

I don't want her to leave, but I'm also not sure what was in Jason's letter. Or what made her think she has to leave right away.

The problem is I can't worry about all that now because we have court today, and we met earlier with Jack to give him the letters to look over. If they need to be used in court, we gave him final say. They are personal, but we both agreed that if it helped River keep her child, so be it.

My stepdad thinks reading them in court today will be the final nail in the coffin to end all this. It will get them in the court records so it's on file in the event they try anything like this again. Not that they have the money to pursue this. I'm not even sure how they have the money to be out here in Montana right now unless Jason's dad took out another loan to do so.

As we enter the courthouse, River clutches onto my hand in fear. I give her a reassuring squeeze while, internally, I'm a ball of nerves. I hoped that the letters would do the trick, but anything could happen in the courtroom.

Jack kicks things off as the court starts.

"Your honor, yesterday my client was visited by a gentleman her late husband served with in the military. He was injured in the same blast that took her husband's life. They knew the situation they were going into was dangerous, so the unit wrote letters to their loved ones. Because of the man's injuries and my client's move, he wasn't able to visit until now. There are three letters I'd like to have read to the court as I believe Jason's parents should hear them as well."

"Objection, we would like to read these in private and decide," the other lawyers say.

"Denied. You have delayed the trial long enough, and I doubt there is anything in the letters that will change my mind on the verdict, but let's see." The judge nods toward Jack.

Jack begins reading Jason's letter to River first, and this is the first time I'm hearing it. River has her eyes on her hands resting in her lap, and tears are pouring down her face.

Next, Jack reads the letter that Jason wrote to me. It's a strange feeling to hear someone's final words to you, especially when they're talking about your mutual love interest. He talks about how he thinks I'm River's soul mate and that he supports us being together.

As the court has no idea how intimate we have been since living together, everyone seems to look at me. They could be judging us or questioning what has happened between us.

Taking a deep breath, I feel exposed under the court's gaze, but I refuse to let my nerves show. Instead, I try to focus on the task at hand. We're here to prove River's fitness as a mother, not to indulge in gossip about our private relationship.

Finally, he reads the letter to Jason's parents.

Mom and Dad,

I'm sorry for not being the son you wanted me to be. You made it clear how disappointed you were in me from the time I was ten and up.

But it was never clearer the day you disowned me for falling in love and following my own path in joining the military and marrying River.

If you don't know by now, River is pregnant with my child. A child who will know nothing but love, something you failed to show me growing up. My child will never wonder if they were a good enough son or daughter to deserve dinner that night. From day one, they will be told they are loved and wanted.

Now that I'm facing being a father, I look back on the meals I wasn't allowed, the beatings I received, the money you stole from me, and I don't know how a parent can treat their child like that.

Just the other day, I made the tough choice that you will never be in my child's life. Not even if you turn up begging to be. I don't ever want them to know you or the kind of 'love' you dish out.

I have found love and have been loved in spite of you, not because of you. I hate to think of the person I would have become if River hadn't stepped into my life and shown me what it was like to be loved and cared for. I might have turned out like you. That would have been the worst thing I could imagine.

The only regret I have in my life is not exposing you as the people you truly are. Karma will deal with you, and just know I will be there to witness it.

Jason

River's sobs fill the courtroom as Jack finishes reading the letter. I place my arm around her in comfort, glaring at Jason's parents with bitter disgust. Their faces remain cold and indifferent, and I wonder how a couple like that could produce such a caring son as Jason.

The judge clears her throat and speaks. "Based on the evidence presented to me today especially, I can confidently say that Mrs. Owens is more than fit to take care of her child. As grandparents to the unborn child, you are not to have any visitation outside of what Mrs. Owns here feels fit to allow you. Which in my opinion, should be nothing. As for the life insurance money. You are not entitled to that, nor would you be, even if you won custody. For the record, the state of Montana isn't a Grandparent's right favorable state, so any appeals on this part of the case will be dismissed," the Judge says. She pauses and takes a breath, then turns to Jack.

"For your counter suit for attorney's fees. I rule in your favor in the amount of fifty thousand dollars. I also rule in favor of the ten thousand dollars for the emotional toll this took on the pregnancy and loss of work she faced while on bed rest."

The judge's gavel crashing down fills the courtroom.

River clings to my arm as we exit the courthouse, her eyes swollen from tears. I can't imagine how she's feeling right now, having just heard her late husband's final words. All I can do is be there for her and offer my support, whatever she needs.

Walking out into the crisp mountain air, I feel a strong sense of relief. It's been a long journey to get to this point, but it's finally over. River's custody of their unborn child is secure, and we can now focus on moving forward.

That relief is short-lived as we walk to the car. Jason's parents follow us out of the courtroom. They are shouting something at us, but their words seem meaningless, lost in the roar of my anger. I turn to face them, my fists clenched at my sides.

Until I hear a squeal from River, I've been so focused on Jason's mom that I don't think to question where Jason's dad is. Before I get a chance to turn, Jason's mom places her hand on my arm and proceeds to faint. Her acting is over-the-top, spiking my senses. Ignoring her, I turn to find Jason's dad gripping River's arm and pulling her backward toward a vehicle as she struggles to get away.

Thankfully, Evan also spots it and is able to get to Mr. Owen's before I can. He has him on the ground in handcuffs as I take River into my arms and move her out of the way.

"You okay, sweetheart?" I ask, watching Jack handcuff Jason's mom with the second cuffs Evan just tossed him.

"Yeah. My arm will be bruised, but otherwise, I'm fine," she says, trembling.

Once the two are in the back of the squad car, Evan comes over to us.

"You okay, River?" he asks, his eyes on her arm.

"Yeah, thanks to you." She smiles at him but never makes a move to leave my arms.

"If you wish to press charges, I can cart them off to jail for you right now. In the state of Montana, harassment such as this, especially right after a case, brings up to five years in jail, per count. Attempted kidnapping is a minimum of two years, but up to one-hundred, depending on what the judge rules. Something like this could be both counts. They could each be spending ten years in jail. I'm sure the judge would love to issue the max penalty if possible," Evan says.

River looks back at me and then places a hand on her stomach. After a moment, she looks back at Evan.

"Yes, officer, I would like to press charges," River says.

Evan nods and steps forward. "Alright then, let's take a ride, folks. You can explain to the judge why you thought it was all right to harass and kidnap a woman who just won custody of her child in court."

Jason's parents look back and forth, unsure of what to do. I can see the fear in their eyes now that they're facing the consequences of their actions. It's a good feeling to see them realize that they can't just bully their way through life.

"I'm going to need you two to join me at the station to give a report, so I can file the paperwork. I'll make it quick because I know River needs to get home and rest after today," Evan says.

Nodding, I help River into the truck and we following him to the police station.

At the station, we give our statements to the police, recounting the events that just happened outside of the courthouse. River details how Jason's dad grabbed her arm and attempted to pull her towards their car. While I explain how I was dealing with his mom who fake fainted to distract me. Evan takes down every word, and I can tell from his expression that he's not impressed with Jason's parents.

Once they have our statements, Evan leads us out of the station and back to the truck. River looks drained as we climb back in, her eyes closed as she leans her head back against the headrest.

"Thank you for being there for me," she whispers.

I reach over and take River's hand in mine, squeezing it gently. "Always," I say softly. "I'll always be here for you." I give her a reassuring smile,

As her eyes flutter open, she asks, "Can we go home now?" Then in a tired whisper, she says, "I just want to go home and rest."

"Of course," I reply, reaching over to start the engine. "Let's get you home."

When we get home, Cole and Jana are there, and the smell of food fills the air.

"Jack caught us leaving and told us what happened. Everyone is glad you're okay and wants to celebrate the win another day. But we figured by the time you got home you would be drained, so we wanted to make you dinner. Lasagna and garlic bread," Jana says hugging River.

"Thank you so much! That sounds perfect after the day we've had," River says.

"Also, Jack asked me to give these back to you. They made copies at the courthouse, but he figured it would mean more for you to have the originals." Cole hands us the letters from Jason.

I take mine and hold it tightly in my hand while River presses her to her chest.

"Thank you. Will you join us for dinner?" she asks.

Cole looks at his wife, and Jana nods.

"We'd love to."

That night, when River goes to bed in her own room, I lay in my bed reading Jason's letter over and over again.

I know beyond anything I want River and I'm not letting her go. I'm going to fight for her. Even Jason knew she was meant to be mine.

CHAPTER 26

RIVER

Today, I have several places in town to look at to rent. The problem is the more I read Jason's letter, the less I want to go. Storm has been acting his old self. Constantly, he's around me, touching me and taking care of me.

He hasn't asked me to stay, nor has there been so much as a kiss. It could all be in my head. Maybe he's just relieved that I'm going to be gone soon, so he's more at ease.

Shaking my head, I try to dispel the hope that rises within me. It's dangerous to entertain the possibility of Jason wanting me to stay. I don't want to get my hopes up, only to have them dashed again.

I head out to the first place on my list, a cozy cabin tucked away in the mountains. As I step inside, I'm immediately hit with the warm aroma of freshly brewed coffee. My heart lifts at the thought of snuggling up with a hot cup of coffee in this charming cabin.

"Hey there! I'm Mia, the landlord," a perky voice calls out.

Turning, I see a petite woman with curly blonde hair and bright blue eyes. She looks friendly and approachable, and I feel a sense of relief wash over me.

"Hi, I'm River," I introduce myself, smiling at her.

Mia beams at me, her eyes lighting up. "It's so nice to meet you, River! Come on in and let me show you around."

When I follow her into the cabin, a strong, pleasant sense of comfort settles over me.

The cabin is cozy and inviting, with soft lighting and warm colors.

"This is the living room, complete with a fireplace and a big, comfy couch," Mia gestures towards the couch with a grin. "Perfect for snuggling up on those cold Montana nights."

I nod, picturing myself curled up on the couch with a good book and a warm blanket. Then suddenly, I have images of being snuggled up with Storm enjoying the warmth of the fire. "It's beautiful," I say, smiling at her.

Mia takes me on a tour of the rest of the cabin, showing me the bedroom, bathroom, and kitchen. Everything is quaint and rustic, with charming touches that make me feel right at home.

When we finish the tour, Mia turns to me with a smile. "So, what do you think?"

"I love it," I say without hesitation. "I have a few other places to look at today, but this is definitely at the top of my list."

We exchange information, and I go downtown to look at an apartment above one of the stores.

But as I walk through the picturesque streets of town, I can feel Storm's gaze on me. How can his presence be palpable even from miles away? Trying to clear my thoughts, I take a deep breath, yet the memories of us together keep flooding back.

I remember the way his hands would roam over my body, the way he would whisper dirty nothings into my ear as we made love under the starry Montana sky. But now, as I ponder over the possibility of leaving for good, a part of me wonders if I would ever feel that way again.

Lost in thought, I accidentally bump into someone and quickly apologize, embarrassed. Glancing up, I find Emelie and Axel.

"River! Are you okay? You were so lost in thought you didn't even hear me calling out," Emelie says.

I laugh, feeling grateful for the distraction. "Sorry about that, just lost in my own head, I guess."

Axel grins at me, swinging an arm around my shoulder. "What's on your mind, River? Maybe we can help. Let's go grab a drink and some desserts at the cafe."

"Well, I won't say no to some hot chocolate," I say, following them to the Cafe a few buildings down.

As we sit at a small table in the cozy cafe, I'm feeling grateful for their company. Emelie and Axel always know how to lift my spirits, and I'm glad to have them as my friends.

"So, what's been going on with you, River?" Emelie asks, taking a sip of her coffee. "Any progress with Storm?"

I feel my cheeks flush at the mention of his name, and my heart rate increases.

"Sadly no. He started to pull back after I had the bleeding episode and was put on bed rest. Then I got the letter from Jason, and I don't know where we are. He's not talking, and I can't seem to figure out if I want to climb the wall or if it's just too big to scale. So, that leaves me out looking at places to live here in town."

My metaphor is horrible, but it's what is on my mind. I don't miss the look Emelie and Axel share before she takes my hand in hers from across the table.

"Love is always worth the risk. Talk to him before you sign anything today. You don't want to live with the regret of what could have been. That will kill your soul slowly, and that isn't what you will want to teach to your child, is it?" Emelie says.

I hate that she's right. Acknowledging her, I nod and take a deep breath as I contemplate her words. She's right, of course. I can't just run away from my problems and leave everything I've ever known behind. In my heart, I know I need to face Storm, confront him about everything that's happened between us, and try to make things right.

"You're right," I say firmly, determination in my voice. "I need to talk to him. Thank you, guys. I don't know what I'd do without you."

Emelie and Axel both smile at me, their support tangible even without words. When I get up to leave, I give them both a huge hug.

From there I go to view the apartment, and it has that homey feel I'm looking to find. Deciding I've seen enough, I drive back to Storm's place. The entire time I'm working on what I'm going to say.

When I pull up, I find him chopping wood over by the barn. Even though I walk over and know he saw me pull up, he keeps working like he doesn't know I'm there.

He stops when I approach and my heart sinks. He doesn't want me here.

"Why are you looking at places, River? Your place is here... with me."

Though, he still is not meeting my eyes.

When I walk over to him, he drops the axe. Not wasting any time, I wrap my arms around him, and he holds me tight.

"I don't want to leave. You are my home. I love you." I tell him and his grip on me tightens.

"I love you too." The emotion in his voice is proof he means every word.

We stand out in the cool air for a while, neither of us wanting to move.

Finally he takes a step back letting me go. "How about we get you inside where it's warm?" He takes my hand, as we walk into the cabin holding hands.

"What changed your mind?" he asks, sitting on the couch with me on his lap.

"Jason's letter. But not for the reasons you might think," I say.

Storm raises an eyebrow, silently urging me to continue. Once again, I take a deep breath, gathering my thoughts before speaking.

"Jason was wrong. He was my soul mate, and I did love him. I just wasn't IN love with him. He was one of those friend soul mates that just gets you. I realized what I felt for you was so much stronger.

Storm's eyes soften as he takes in my words, a small smile playing on his lips. "I'm glad to hear that. Because I love you too, River. More than anything."

As his words rush over me, I feel a weight lifted off my shoulders. This is where I'm meant to be. I know it in my spirit that he's it for me. My heart is full as I lean in to kiss him, feeling his arms wrap around me tightly.

"You about took me to the edge of my sanity walking out the door this morning," he says.

"Then I guess it's time for you to take me to the edge." I move my hips to brush over his growing hard on. We fit perfectly.

He smiles at me, his eyes alight, and I know that everything will be okay. We'll make it through this and be better for it. Storm and I will be our own kind of epic love story.

CHAPTER 27

STORM

It's been a few weeks since River won against Jason's parents, and we put off our friends as long as we could about having a celebration party. Finally, Emelie insisted we turn it into a baby shower instead.

This is River and my first time out of the cabin, other than for doctor's appointments. Since we admitted our feelings for each other, we have pretty much used that time to really get to know each other, talk, and plan.

There is a lot for her to get to know about prepping for winter up here. Then, there's so much to discuss about life with the baby and making both detailed and contingency plans. Also, we have been moving things around the house, getting set to bring her stuff up from storage before winter kicks in.

Today, we are gathered at Emelie and Axel's place, and everyone is here, even Evan.

River looks beautiful as always, her pregnancy bringing out a glow in her, which makes me never wanting to take my eyes off of her.

Sitting next to River on the couch, I watch her open gifts for our unborn child. Looking around me, I feel a surge of overwhelming gratitude for the family we've built here in the Montana mountains. It's been a long road to get here, but with River by my side, I feel like we can conquer anything life throws our way.

I have big plans for today, and Axel and Emelie know about it. They helped me plan it, so as she opens each gift my nerves ramp up more and more.

As River unwraps a set of soft, woolen baby blankets, I smile and reach for her hand.

Her eyes flicker up to mine, and I can see the love and trust she has for me shining in their depths.

"Okay, River, there's one more gift left," I say. My heart is thumping in my chest as I reach under the couch cushion to retrieve a small velvet box. "This one's from me."

All eyes are on us as I take River's hand in mine and slide off the couch to one knee on the floor in front of her. Then, opening the box, I show her a small, sparkling diamond ring.

River gasps as I hold up the ring, her hand flying up to her chest as she stares at the diamond. The anticipation and nervousness is building up inside of me, waiting for her to say something.

"Storm, I--" she starts, but I cut her off by sliding the ring onto her finger.

"River, I love you more than anything in this world. I know we've been through a lot, but I want to spend the rest of my life with you, as your partner and as the father of this child," I say, taking her other hand in mine.

"We can take as long as you want to plan this wedding, but I want to know that you are mine and that this is our future. Will you marry me?"

River stares at the ring for a moment, her eyes glistening with tears. I can see her mind racing, the weight of my proposal bearing down on her.

Finally, she looks up at me, and the love and adoration that she holds for me is in her gaze. Her eyes fill with tears as she opens her mouth to speak. "Yes, of course, I'll marry you."

Relief floods through me as I hear her answer, and I'm feeling as if I'm on top of the world. Slowly, I stand, pulling River along with me as our friends and family cheer and applaud.

The women take River off to stare at the ring and talk wedding plans. While the guys gather around to congratulate me.

"Thanks for making me the last single guy in the group. Emelie is already trying to set me up with people," Evan says.

"Well, she wants everyone to be as happy as she is. I don't blame her. So, *is* there anyone in your life?" I ask, poking at him.

"I don't know. She isn't from here, and I doubt she will stay," he says, not giving anything away.

"A tourist?" I ask shocked.

"No. God no. It's work related," he whispers furtively.

Evan likes someone at work who he's in to, but she doesn't live here. My guess it's one of the State people. They sometime pop into town now and then for cases or to do reviews.

As I continue to chat with the guys, my mind wanders back to River. I've gotten used to having her so close the last few weeks that even on the other end of the house seems too much.

I make my way over to where the women are gathered. As I approach, River looks up and sees me, a smile spreading across her face. "Hey," she says, reaching out to take my hand. "We were just talking about wedding plans. Emelie's already offered to help with the decorations."

Nodding, I smile back at her. I love seeing her smile and settling in so well with the life I built here.

When I sit down next to River, a beautiful, peaceful feeling washes over me. It's not just because we're engaged, but also because of the baby we're going to have. It's going to be tough, but it will also be worth it. Our love can conquer anything. I truly believe that.

"Have you thought about where you want to have the wedding?" I ask her, turning to face her.

She smiles at me, her eyes lighting up. "I was thinking we could have it on our property. We could set up a beautiful outdoor wedding, right in the meadow, with the mountain as our backdrop."

"Do you want the fall leaves as the backdrop or spring flowers?" Emelie says already scribbling in a notebook.

Since she knew about the proposal, she was ready to jump into planning mode.

"Spring, I think. I don't want to be pregnant in my photos."

"Whatever you want, sweetheart. I think you would look beautiful either way. There is a huge patch of wildflowers behind the house that bloom in spring. They will make a gorgeous backdrop for our photos, too," I tell her, sending the women off in another flurry of planning.

It's still another two hours before I'm able to pull River away and go home.

As River and I drive home, I'm feeling appreciative for everything we have. I look over at her, her hand resting on her belly, and I can see the love in her eyes. Reaching over, I take her hand, giving it a gentle squeeze. "I can't wait to spend the rest of my life with you," I say. My voice is filled with emotion as I pull into the driveway and park the truck.

"I feel the same way," she replies, turning to look at me. "I love you, Storm."

"I love you too, River," I say, leaning in to kiss her.

Going into *our* home, I can feel the excitement building inside of me. We have so much to plan for our future together, and it's a feeling like no other. Leading River inside, my heart pounds as I close the door behind us.

My body is buzzing with anticipation as we settle on the couch. We're engaged now, and everything feels different. More exciting, more meaningful, more... everything. I reach out and take River's hand again, gazing into her eyes.

She smiles back at me, her cheeks flushed with excitement. I lean in to kiss her again, the passion between us growing stronger with every passing moment. Our lips meet, and my heart races with desire. Wrapping my arms around her, I pull her even closer to me.

For the first time in my life, I feel truly alive. River is everything to me, and I can't wait to spend the rest of my life with her. I know that there will be challenges along the way, but with her by my side, we can conquer anything that comes our way.

Epilogue

River

1 year later

"Hey, where is the little man?" Storm asks, walking in from the barn where he's been hauling firewood in to keep it dry all morning.

"He's still napping. Though he should be waking up anytime now. With him teething, he fought sleep pretty hard."

As usual, whenever he can, he pulls me into a kiss. When Storm breaks away from the kiss, I look up into his eyes and smile.

It's been just over a year since we moved out to this remote part of Montana, and every day feels like a dream come true.

Unable to help myself, I run my hand through his hair before leaning in for another kiss. As our lips touch, his arms wrap around me, pulling me closer to his body.

Suddenly, we hear a sound coming from the bedroom. We break away from the kiss and go towards the room to find our son awake. He sees Storm and starts smiling.

Storm picks up our son and throws him up in the air, making him laugh even harder. I smile at the two of them, feeling my heart swell with love. I can't believe how blessed I am to have these two in my life.

When I went into labor, I was terrified. But Storm was calm, and our friends rallied around us. Surprisingly, when I didn't have the strength to keep going, I felt Jason there pushing me on. Our son came in to the world in the early hours kicking and screaming.

After some talk, we named him Jason George Owens and named Jason as the father on his birth certificate. Storm wanted to find a way to honor his stepdad, who has always been there for him, and I couldn't think of a better way to do so.

When his mom and stepdad came into the room to meet the baby, we told them the name. Until then, it had been a secret. That grown man cried so hard, there wasn't a dry eye in the room even from the nurse who was taking my vitals.

After we got home and settled, Storm started the process of adopting Jason officially. Thanks to the legal fees Jack buried Jason's parents under and the charges Evan placed on them, they not have the money to fight the adoption process. They couldn't even do anything from their jail cells. So, the adoption went through last month, and the judge asked why we didn't just name Storm the dad on the birth certificate. Storm had the perfect answer. He said that putting his name on the birth certificate would be erasing Jason's father. He never wants to do that.

Storm said his stepdad honored his father, and he wants to do the same.

That was all the judge needed because he granted the adoption with no further questions asked.

Storm looks at our son with so much love and adoration in his eyes that tears well up in my eyes. I never thought I could feel such love and happiness, but being here with my family makes every day feel like a blessing.

As Storm plays with Jason, I walk over to the window, gazing out at the stunning view of the Montana mountains. The snow-capped peaks shimmer in the sunlight, and the trees seem to dance in the gentle breeze. I take a deep breath of the fresh mountain air, feeling a familiar sense of peace settle over me.

This is the same view we had as the backdrop to our wedding this past spring. We were married in a small ceremony while the wildflowers were in bloom.

I turn around to find Storm watching me with a soft smile on his lips. "What are you thinking about?" he asks, walking over to me and wrapping his arm around my waist.

"I'm just thinking about how lucky we are," I answer, resting my head on his shoulder.

"I know, right?" he says, pressing a kiss to my temple. "I never thought I could be this happy."

"Me neither," I reply, feeling contentment wash over me.

"You need to get ready. My parents will be here any minute," Storm says.

Glancing at the time, I can see he's right. I need to start getting ready.

Normally I have lunch in town with his mom, but today we are having family dinner so they can see Jason.

Before we even announced we were engaged, both his parents took to me as if I was their own daughter. I couldn't ask for better in laws. Both of them are my friends, making our relationship perfect. I talk with Storm's mom all the time and we have lunch together once a week.

Usually, she comes to Whiskey River for lunch, but sometimes we go to see them for the day. Recently, his mom and stepdad talked to us as about the plans they are making for when George's term is over. It's no surprise that they want to move to Whiskey River to be closer to their grandchild. Their words, they think of Jason as their grandchild, and that's exactly how they treat him.

They gave this whole spiel on how they know Storm moved out here to be on his own and how they didn't want to be a bother. They would live in town and wouldn't stop by unannounced. But Storm smiled through it and in the end said he'd love to have them so close.

Last month they bought a piece of land on the edge of town and will be building their forever home on it. It's a good half hour drive from our place to theirs, so plenty of buffer space, as his mom keeps saying.

While I get dinner ready, I'm thrilled and excited at the thought of having Storm's parents closer to us. It's always been a dream of mine to have a close-knit family, and it feels like we're slowly building that here in the Montana mountains.

I was just putting my hair up when Storm walks into the bathroom, dressed in his nicest flannel and a pair of jeans that fit him just right. He looks at me through the mirror, his eyes tracing over my figure. "You look beautiful," he says, giving me a soft smile.

Turning to face him, I feel a blush creep up my cheeks. "Thank you," I reply, warmth and happiness spreading through me.

He leans in, pressing a soft kiss to my lips. "Let's go meet my parents," he says, taking my hand and leading me out of the bathroom.

Jason is in his playpen, watching one of his cartoons and laughing at the TV. He doesn't even look up at the knock on the door or at the dogs all barking.

When we brought Jason home, Shadow took right to him and pretty much never leaves his side. So, while his ears perk up and he watches the door to see who it is, he doesn't move from his spot beside the playpen Jason is in.

The greetings for Storm and I are short and rushed because they want to get right over and see Jason. Storm's mom picks him up and I know she won't put him down again until she leaves.

"Oh, don't forget to light that candle you got. Mom you will love the scent. It's a perfect fall candle that we picked it up in town last week," Storm says.

Going to the fireplace, I light it before setting it back in the middle. On either side of the candle are photos. I've placed both mine and Jason's wedding photo there, along with Storm and my wedding photo. Several other photos adorn the mantle, including Jason, Storm, and me over the years, and the most recent is of our trip to Arlington.

Storm kept his promise, and when the doctor cleared me and Jason to fly, he took us to Arlington so Jason could meet his son. Then we told our son the amazing story of the man who did everything he could to protect him. We got some photos, and Storm made us a promise that day. We'd come out at least twice a year, one of them being for Jason's birth, which just happens to be a week after his son's.

The walls of our home are filled with our son's photo, but this mantle is dedicated to the man who brought us together and is the whole reason our little family exists at all.

As we sit down for dinner, Storm's mom starts to chat excitedly about the progress they've made on their new home. Mostly they just got the land cleared and are working on the floor plan drawings. "It's so exciting to finally be building our dream home," she says, taking a sip of her wine. "And we can't wait to be so close to you guys and little Jason."

George nods in agreement. "Plus, we'll finally have a good excuse to come visit more often." He winks at me, making me grin.

We spend the rest of the evening chatting about our plans for the future and reminiscing about old times. Storm's mom tells us about how she's already planning a big family Thanksgiving dinner at their new home next year. Not for the first time, I enjoy the warmth that spreads through me at the thought of having a big, close-knit family gathering.

After dinner, Storm's parents head back to their hotel, and we tuck Jason into bed. As I crawl into bed beside Storm, he turns to me with a mischievous glint in his eyes. "You know, now that my parents are going to be living so close, we might have a little more alone time," he says, his lips curling into a smirk.

I giggle, feeling a sense of excitement start to build within me. "Is that right?" I tease, feeling a shiver run down my spine as Storm's hand trails up my thigh. "Well, we wouldn't want to waste any opportunities for alone time," I say, flipping over to straddle him and lean down to capture his lips with mine.

After all, how else will we give Jason a brother or sister?

·•·•••••·

Want a Bonus Epilogue of Storm and River? **Make sure to sign up for my newsletter to grab it!**

Grab Detective Evan Greer's Book next in **Take Me To The Valley.**

OTHER BOOKS BY KACI ROSE

See all of Kaci Rose's Books

Mountain Men of Whiskey River

Take Me To The River – Axel and Emelie

Take Me To The Cabin – Pheonix and Jenna

Take Me To The Lake – Cash and Hope

Taken by The Mountain Man - Cole and Jana

Take Me To The Mountain – Bennett and Willow

Take Me To The Cliff – Jack and Sage

Take Me To The Edge – Storm and River

Take Me To The Valley

Oakside Military Heroes Series

Saving Noah – Lexi and Noah

Saving Easton – Easton and Paisley

Saving Teddy – Teddy and Mia

Saving Levi – Levi and Mandy

Saving Gavin – Gavin and Lauren

Saving Logan – Logan and Faith

Saving Zane

Oakside Shorts

Saving Mason - Mason and Paige

Saving Ethan – Bri and Ethan

Club Red – Short Stories

Daddy's Dare – Knox and Summer

Sold to my Ex's Dad - Evan and Jana

Jingling His Bells – Zion and Emma

Watching You – Ella and Brooks, Connor, and Finn

Club Red: Chicago

Elusive Dom - Carter and Gemma

Forbidden Dom – Gage and Sky

Mountain Men of Mustang Mountain

(Series Written with Dylann Crush and Eve London)
February is for Ford – Ford and Luna
April is For Asher – Asher and Jenna
June is for Jensen – Jensen and Courtney
August is for Ace – Ace and Everly
October is for Owen – Owen and Kennedy
December is for Dean – Dean and Holly

Mustang Mountain Riders
(Series Written with Eve London)
February's Ride With Bear
April's Ride With Stone
June's Ride With Lightning
August's Ride With Arrow
October's Ride With Atlas
December's Ride With Scar

Chasing the Sun Duet

Sunrise – Kade and Lin

Sunset – Jasper and Brynn

Rock Stars of Nashville

She's Still The One – Dallas and Austin

Accidental Series

Accidental Sugar Daddy – Owen and Ellie

The Billionaire's Accidental Nanny - Mari and Dalton

The Italian Mafia Princesses

Midnight Rose - Ruby and Orlando

Standalone Books

Texting Titan - Denver and Avery

Stay With Me Now – David and Ivy

Committed Cowboy – Whiskey Run Cowboys

Stalking His Obsession - Dakota and Grant

Falling in Love on Route 66 - Weston and Rory

CONNECT WITH KACI ROSE

Website

Kaci Rose's Book Shop

Facebook

Kaci Rose Reader's Facebook Group

TikTok

Instagram

Twitter

Goodreads

Book Bub

Join Kaci Rose's VIP List (Newsletter)

About Kaci Rose

Kaci Rose writes steamy contemporary romances mostly set in small towns. She grew up in Florida but now lives in a cabin in the mountains of East Tennessee.

She is a mom to 5 kids, a rescue dog who is scared of his own shadow, an energetic young German Shepard who is still in training, A sleepy old hound who adopted her, and a reluctant indoor cat. Kaci loves to travel, and her goal is to visit all 50 states before she turns 50. She has 17 more to

go, mostly in the Midwest and on the West
Coast!

She also writes steamy cowboy romances as
Kaci M. Rose.

PLEASE LEAVE A REVIEW!

I love to hear from my readers! Please **head over to your favorite store and leave a review** of what you thought of this book! Reviews also appreciated on BookBub and Goodreads!

Made in United States
North Haven, CT
22 June 2024

53927126R00196